SOMETHING
REAL

SOMETHING REAL

NEW YORK TIMES BESTSELLING AUTHOR

LEXI RYAN

DEDICATION

Dedicated to Brian. Again and always. They're all for you.

PROLOGUE

Liz

HE LOWERS HIS MOUTH to mine, and at first I don't react. It's as if my brain is too busy trying to make sense of the noise in my head, and it can't be bothered to process the impossible-to-believe. Because "Sam's father is kissing me" is about as easy to digest as someone screaming, "Run, that Yeti is gonna get you!"

This has to be one of those crazy dreams I have. Like the one where I find myself having sex with the guy who cuts my turkey at the supermarket deli. I don't stop it in the dream because I'm not really making conscious decisions.

But when Travis Bradshaw sweeps his tongue against my lips, I snap back to reality and push him away, shoving him hard with both hands. He steps away, his face twisted into a grimace, then he turns his back to me.

My stomach roils and fills with that sick feeling of too many emotions at once. Shame, guilt, betrayal, regret, anger, loss, and, yeah, disgust. This man, the father of the man I love, the politician I once respected—my *boss*—disgusts me. I can't separate one emotion from another, and they all pile onto one another in a glob of paralyzing fear.

"How long have you known it was me?" I ask. Of all the questions and angry accusations swirling through my head, I'm not sure why that's the first out of my mouth.

"A while." He shoves his hands into his pockets and looks out the window. "I wasn't looking for an affair, Elizabeth. I never meant for this to happen. But you and I just . . . we clicked. By the time I looked up your profile and saw who you were, I didn't know what to do."

"So you . . . what? Offered me a job?" The truth is a hard fist to my stomach. "It was never about you thinking I had talent. You never thought I was *smart enough* to work your campaign. You just wanted . . . what did you want? What did you think would happen?"

He spins back around, his face angry. "I would have given you *anything*. You wanted a job, so I gave you one. You wanted to feel important, so I gave you important work. You're welcome, by the way."

"You should have ended it when you found out who

I was. You should have told me. You should have . . ."

"Should have what? Should have known that you would let *me* get you all hot and bothered and then go fuck my *son*?"

I throw my hand over my mouth. I'm really going to throw up. I didn't know horror could cause literal nausea. I thought that was just something people said. "If I was turned on by our conversations—"

"*If?*"

"It was only because I thought I was talking to Sam. You knew this wasn't okay and you let me . . . you had to have known I'd be upset when I found out."

"I wanted to tell you the truth. That's why I invited you to the cabin."

But he was at the hospital, waiting for his first grandchild to be delivered. And Sam showed up at the cabin instead.

My stomach rolls. When I close my eyes, I see Sam looking down at me, telling me he loves me. *Loved* me. He couldn't love me after this. I've lost him. "You ruined everything."

"I've arranged for you to have a position as a staffer on Christine's campaign. In exchange for your promise to never speak of this, I'll pay you—"

"*Pay me?* I don't want your money."

"You could destroy me."

A car door slams, and I draw in a horrified breath at the sight of Sam's car out the window. "You've already destroyed *me*," I whisper. I should run. I should get out of here before Sam walks in. But my feet won't work, and I can't seem to peel myself away from the safety of the wall.

The front door chimes merrily, only making the booming footsteps coming toward this office sound all the more ominous.

"You'll take the money," Sam's father says. Any kindness or tenderness that was in his eyes before is gone now. These are the hard eyes of a calculating businessman. "And you'll keep this quiet."

The office door swings open, and the room rattles as it slams into the wall.

Sam's eyes blaze with confusion and anger as he looks at his father, then me, then back. He takes three long steps and swings. There's a horrible crack as his knuckles connect with his father's jaw.

Sam

Dad takes a step forward, fists rising, but then he stops himself and stares at me. That special brand of paternal disapproval is clear in his eyes.

"Liz, leave us, please," Dad says, never taking his eyes from me.

"Sam," Liz says. My name sounds more like a squeak than a word, and yet there's so much emotion packed into that single syllable that I flinch.

"Go, Liz." My fist is on fire, a sharp contrast to the empty void in my chest.

"Just let me—"

"You've done enough."

She flinches, then nods and scurries out the door.

"You ruin everything," I tell him. The fire spreads up my fingers and into my arm in sharp tingles. "Everything." I open my mouth to say more, but the numbness is fading entirely now, creeping toward my chest. I feel as if I might burst open if I say more, so I leave it at that, and I go.

Liz is out front, her face white, her arms wrapped around herself. "I didn't know it was him."

"But it was."

"I thought it was you, then I thought it was Connor. I had no idea it was your dad."

"You thought you'd been talking to *Connor*? Is that supposed to make me feel better?"

"Not at first. I—"

I hold up a hand. "Just stop talking."

"The morning at the cabin. I thought it was you. River messaged me. I thought it was Connor." She's not making sense, and judging by the panic on her face, she knows it. "Once I knew it wasn't you, I thought . . . I was sure . . . and I was going to quit, but you . . . the governor . . . You have to believe me."

My jaw aches from clenching my teeth. "I can't listen to this."

"I *love* you. You. Love. Me." Her eyes are pleading, desperate.

The hot iron in my stomach turns icy, and cold anger spreads through my gut that radiates out through my limbs. "That doesn't matter anymore. How am I

5

supposed to trust you now?"

"I swear this wasn't my fault. Can we just . . . can we talk somewhere?"

"You knew you were talking to a married man, but you didn't do anything about it. And last summer when you slept with Connor, you knew he was with Della."

"I didn't—"

"I've heard enough." I turn toward my car and reach for the door handle. Liz grabs my arm, and I freeze. "Let go of me." My voice sounds cold, even to my own ears.

"I need to explain."

I shake off her hand and open the car door. "I can't even look at you."

CHAPTER ONE

Sam
Five Months Later...

My FIRST THOUGHT when the doorbell rings is *maybe that's Liz.*

And that's just how pathetic I am—hoping for the woman I love to come to my door and tell me she can't live without me, even though I was a complete and total dick, and God knows there's no future for us. But the thought's there, and like it or not, it's the driving force that has me putting down my scotch when I otherwise wouldn't bother to answer.

I'm not exactly sober, but I'm definitely not drunk

enough, because when I pull open my door, who's standing there but my motherfucking asshole brother-in-law?

"Fuck off," I mutter, swinging the door closed.

He catches it with his foot. "We have a problem."

I glare at Connor, daring him to . . . what? I don't know. I wish he'd throw a punch or something so I'd have an excuse to start swinging. While I'm not typically an angry drunk, tonight I'd take any opportunity to go a few rounds.

There better be a goddamn fantastic reason he's here. I have very important plans for my Thursday night, and they involve drinking scotch until I can't feel my face. Because it's been five months since I found out the woman I loved was having an illicit online affair with my father. Five months since I punched my own father in the face and stopped speaking to him altogether.

Five months since she left.

"Sam." Connor says my name like an apology. As if he feels *sorry* for me, just for the fact that I have to be me.

Join the fucking club, buddy.

I don't bother answering or trying to kick him out of my house. I turn around and head back to my couch. And my scotch.

The glass is halfway to my lips when he sits next to me and takes it from my hand. "It's important."

"If this is about my father's campaign, you're wasting your time. You know how many shits I give about his chances of moving into the governor's mansion? Zero shits, Connor. I give zero shits about the mansion or the office or, let's be clear, about my father."

Sighing, he lifts the tumbler to his lips and shoots it back, grimacing as it goes down. *Pussy.*

He exhales slowly. "This isn't about your father. It's about you." He taps the screen on his phone a few times then hands it over to me. "You and these pictures, which are going to air on the national evening news tonight, if you even care."

Liz

"Let me help you with those."

I loop the sixth and final grocery bag over my arm and turn to see my neighbor standing beside my car.

"Hi." I realize I don't know his name, even though we've seen each other nearly every morning for the past five months.

He grins. "Hi." Today, he's in a fitted black T-shirt, his hands tucked into his pockets, his dark, wild hair slipping to cover his left eye. Before I can say anything, he's taking the bags from my hands. My biceps and forearms sing with relief.

He sweeps his gaze down my body in a way that leaves me flushed, but the warmth has barely had a chance to settle in before I go cold with guilt. Sam and I may not be together anymore, we may not have a fighting chance to ever be together again, but even the thought of letting another man look at me like that feels like a betrayal.

"Is this all of it?" he asks. His biceps bulge as he lifts the bags.

I'm capable of carrying in my own groceries, but I'm just lonely enough that I can't resist his offer, misplaced guilt be damned. "You don't have to do that." The words ring empty.

"Oh, but I do," he says. "I'm shamelessly using your groceries as an excuse to get your name. Mine's George."

I sink my teeth into my bottom lip. George is cute. Tall, dark, broad-shouldered, and with a smile that makes me blush. He has a great smile. This isn't the first time I've noticed. I should be so hot for this guy, but I'm not exactly in a place for dating, emotionally speaking.

"Liz," I answer. "Thanks for helping."

He leads the way, and I unlock the door when we reach the top of the stairs. Letting him carry in my groceries feels like a treat and a sin, and I hate that I feel guilty for accepting a simple kindness.

"Can I get you something to drink? I have water, diet soda, and coffee." I also have vodka, tequila, and beer, but no how, no way, am I going to drink around a handsome man when I'm feeling this lonely and sorry for myself. I've made that mistake before.

"Why don't I make the coffee while you put away the groceries?" he asks.

I nod, and we work side by side in companionable, if somewhat awkward silence until my groceries have been put in their places and the smell of coffee is filling my small apartment.

I pull a couple of mugs from the cabinet, then find the sugar and cream as he pours us each a cup. "Do you take anything in yours?" I ask.

He shakes his head and watches me as I doctor my coffee with a good quarter cup of sugar and matching amounts of cream. "I'm not sure what that is," he says, a grin tugging on the corner of his mouth as he studies my cup, "but it's no longer coffee."

I wrap my cold hands around the mug. I won't take more than a sip or two. My stomach can't handle much coffee these days. Or food, for that matter. It's too busy eating itself to let me eat anything else. I've lost seven pounds since Christmas.

Body by guilt and self-loathing.

"So, tell me about yourself, George." I force a smile and place my coffee on the counter. A handsome man just carried up my groceries. The least I can do is make some polite conversation. "What do you do?"

"I work for an online magazine. Programming, mostly. If you're avoiding that coffee because you're worried the caffeine will keep you up, let me tell you about what I did at work last week. You'll fall asleep in no time."

That earns a giggle from me, and the sound feels so unnatural coming from my mouth that I wonder when I last laughed.

"What about you?" He holds up a hand. "No, let me

guess. I'm good at this. You're . . . a lion tamer?"

I grin. "How'd you guess?"

"Oh, you know, you just have that fierce but tenacious look about you. It's pretty obvious, really."

"Fierce but tenacious. Can't say anyone's ever described me that way before." I attempt a sip and feel the smile fall from my face. *Stop thinking about Sam. Nothing good down that road.* I force myself to give my attention to the man in the room rather than the one who consumes my mind. "Truth be told," I say, "I'm no longer a lion tamer. I retired young in favor of starting a second career."

"Tricky," he says. He narrows his eyes. "Law professor."

I snort. "What about me says, 'law professor'?" If only I were smart enough for something like that.

He grins. "Fierce but tenacious, remember? My mother's a law professor, so I know the type well. But I can tell by your face you think that's a terrible career choice—and my mother would probably agree—so let me guess again . . . If only your choice of wardrobe could provide me with a hint."

I glance down at my "Guy for President" T-shirt. Under Guy's logo, the shirt says, "Staffer." I sigh. "I'm an enigma wrapped in a mystery. Or is it a mystery wrapped in an enigma?"

"I have a hunch you're more than that. Would you join me for dinner some time, and let me find out?"

That question from a guy like this—cute and funny—should make my day. Instead, I realize I'm looking for an excuse to decline his offer. I feel nothing. Nothing but the ache that's been eating me alive from the moment Sam punched his father and turned his tortured eyes on me.

"I can't even look at you."

I don't know how to explain. I left New Hope five months ago and moved into this little apartment on the north side of Indy. After five months, I should be able to move on. I want to like him. I want to give him a chance, to fall in love and forget I ever lost my heart to a man who hates me. "George, you're a really nice guy . . ."

George winces. "A *nice* guy? Ouch. If you were going to turn me down, I was hoping you'd do it with something more like, 'You're so dead sexy, I fear I couldn't control myself around you.' It's not too late. Try that one."

I laugh fully this time. "Oh, but now you won't believe me."

"I promise to forget I'm the one who suggested it." He takes a sip of his coffee and sighs as he looks at me through thick, dark lashes. When I think he's not going to say anything more, he asks, "Who is he?"

"What?"

"The guy who broke your heart. Was he a boyfriend? First love?" He drops his gaze to my left hand. "Husband?"

"He didn't break . . ." I shake my head. "Boyfriend. And I'm not sure it's fair to say he broke my heart. It was kind of my fault."

"Ah, but your heart *is* broken, and he's the reason."

"I guess so. Yeah."

"Well, if you're ever interested in trying to think about someone else for an evening, I'd love to help you out."

"I'll think about it." But I won't. Not really. Not when the invitation makes me realize just how badly I need to send Sam the letter in my purse. It's been there for weeks, and tomorrow morning, I'm going to mail it. It's time.

CHAPTER TWO

Liz

"THE TWINS ARE CRAWLING everywhere and getting into everything," Hanna says around a yawn. "I think they're going to start walking soon too, and God help us all when that happens. I don't know if I should do more baby proofing or buy those leash things people put on their children."

I laugh. My nieces, Sophie and Josie, are little hellions who think they can get away with anything because of their cherubic smiles. They're only right ninety-five percent of the time. "If you put my girls in leashes, I'm bringing them to live here with Aunt

Lizzy."

Hanna snorts. "Deal." Her long brown hair falls in messy, loose waves around her shoulders and her cheeks are flushed, as if I just woke her from a nap with my video-chat call.

"Are they letting you sleep?" I ask. "You look a little tired."

She blushes. "The girls aren't the problem," she says, giving a pointed look to someone off-camera. "He's hardly let me sleep since he's been home from the last leg of his tour."

"I can hear you," says Nate, Hanna's husband, from the background.

"Haven't you two had enough of each other yet?"

Hanna ducks her head, and again I hear my brother-in-law. "Never."

"You hanging in there?" she asks. "We miss you."

"I'm fine. I'm learning so much with the campaign." It's a white lie, but maybe one of those things that will feel true a year from now when I look back on these months. "I've never lived anywhere but New Hope. This is good for me. I don't have someone to come to my rescue every time something is hard."

"There's nothing wrong with always having someone who will rescue you," Hanna says. "We're here, okay? Just don't forget that. You don't have to do this alone."

"I know." But the truth is, they have their own lives. They have their own problems and their own families. Cally and Hanna have new babies. Krystal is running the management side of the bakery for Hanna. And even though Maggie doesn't have any children of her own yet, Asher's daughter, Zoe, is hers in all the ways that count, and since they started sending Zoe to school in New Hope, she now spends more time with Maggie and Asher than with her mom in New York. While Nix is still single, and is probably the most like me in terms of loneliness, she's a doctor and her thriving practice keeps her busy.

I'm not upset with my sisters and best friend for settling down and having kids. I'm disappointed I'm not doing it with them.

It's better that I'm here.

"Has Princess been adopted?" I ask. I miss my visits to the New Hope Humane Shelter and the dogs there, but I especially miss Princess.

"Not yet. I went by the shelter yesterday to visit her. She's doing well."

I wish I could adopt her, but since I don't know where I'll be living or what I'll be doing when I'm no longer working on Guy's campaign, I'm not sure that's a good idea.

"So, how's work?" Hanna asks.

I shrug. "Oh, you know. Another day, another sorority girl calling me a bitch because I won't lie about her volunteer hours for her Poli-Sci class."

"You could come home." She smiles to soften the suggestion. She knows she says it too often, but that doesn't stop her.

"I miss you too, and don't worry. I promised Mom I'd be there for church this weekend."

"You should come home tonight and go out with me

and the girls! We'll go to Brady's, like old times." I struggle to keep my face neutral, but Hanna backpedals anyway. "*Or* we could stay in. Drink, play cards, or something. It would be fun. Of course, if we don't want to drink in front of little ones, we'd need to go to Nix's new house or Krystal's apartment, but I'm sure they wouldn't mind."

"Angel!" Nate calls from the background. Hanna turns her head, and I'm saved from having to respond to the invitation. Guy's presidential campaign headquarters is in Indianapolis, so the drive back to New Hope isn't terrible, but the risk of seeing Sam is.

When Hanna turns back to the screen, her face has gone pale. "Liz, maybe you should turn on the news. WCBF."

"Okay . . ." I grab the remote off the end table, click on the TV, and dial into the national network.

"I'm so sorry," Hanna says.

I blink at the screen, but the scrolling headline doesn't make any sense to me.

"Honey, are you okay?" Hanna asks.

I shake my head and turn up the volume on my television.

"Due to their sexually graphic nature, WCBF has chosen to black out large portions of the images, but we strongly encourage our viewers to have their children leave the room. If you're sensitive to such materials, please be advised."

The screen fills with an image of the nude woman on her knees, hands bound behind her back, hair in the fist of a faceless man. Her face isn't visible, but her long red hair and porcelain-pale skin instantly make me think of Sabrina Guy, my boss's daughter.

Like the first, the next image doesn't show either face. The woman is tied to a bed, arms about her head, a muscled male form hovering over her.

"Since when did the six o'clock news start featuring pornography?" Hanna grumbles.

I already know what I'm looking at—*who* I'm looking at—but if I wanted to deny the truth to myself, the final image takes away any choice. It shows the same woman and the same muscled male body, but in this one, the face of the man is clear.

I draw in an involuntary gasp. I want to look away, but I can't take my eyes off Samuel Bradshaw's face. Then that incomprehensible headline rolls past again: *Sabrina Guy "tied up" in sex-tape scandal with on-again, off-again boyfriend Samuel Bradshaw.*

"What are we looking at here?" the newscaster asks his guest "expert." Expert at what, I'm not sure. Can you go to college and major in regrettable sex photos? Does the homework require you to watch the Paris Hilton sex tape?

"These are still shots from a sex tape that was leaked to my magazine, *Stars Like Us,*" the journalist says. "At first, we didn't think much of it. The redheaded woman in the video could be anyone, and we don't get a good enough shot of her face to identify her. But beyond the woman bearing a striking resemblance to Governor Guy's daughter, Sabrina, a closer look at the background reveals a few interesting things." The screen flips back to the first image. "You see that bronze bust in the background there?" The screen zooms in on that part of the image. "That's a trophy for the Woman Leader of the Year, awarded to Christine Guy a decade ago and known to be in the library of the Guys' country home. Then if we look at the final image . . ." The image on the screen changes to the one showing Sam's face. "Here we can see the face of the young man she's with, Samuel Bradshaw, son of Travis Bradshaw, candidate for governor of Indiana."

"Now introducing WCBF's political analyst, Rhea Lane, to give her take on this situation," the newscaster says. "Do you agree that the man in the picture appears to be Samuel Bradshaw?"

"I do," the analyst says. "Although Bradshaw himself couldn't be reached for comment, a friend of the family has identified him. A relationship between Bradshaw and Candidate Guy's daughter wouldn't be a big surprise, since the Bradshaws and the Guys have been friends for years. The Bradshaws were strong financial backers for Guy's gubernatorial campaign, and Guy's endorsement of Bradshaw almost guarantees him the spot as Indiana's next governor. But his son's tape with Guy's daughter could cost Christine her chance at the White House."

My stomach lurches, threatening to bring up the two sips of coffee I had while George was here, and my face pales on the chat screen.

"Who *cares* who he screws?" Hanna says. As much as I appreciate her righteous indignation on my behalf, I wish we weren't on this video chat right now. If I have to find out the man I love is having kinky sex with some other woman, I'd rather not have my twin looking on while I digest the information.

"With final primaries in Montana and South Dakota in just over a week," the analyst continues, "it's fair to say this will be a blow to Candidate Guy's votes from her more conservative supporters. It's been a hotly contested race between Guy and Candidate Roe, but many people believed Roe would be giving his concession speech next week. Now that's not so clear."

"Can we be sure the people in this picture are Sabrina Guy and Samuel Bradshaw?" the newscaster asks.

"We contacted Guy headquarters before the broadcast, and they declined to comment, but Samuel and Sabrina have been seen together at many political events and fundraisers over the years. It's not much of a leap to assume their relationship has expanded to one behind closed doors."

"But their relationship isn't really the concern here, is it?" the newscaster asks.

"Exactly. During Guy's second term as governor, Sabrina's been touring the public schools on an 'I'm Worth Waiting For' campaign that's all about waiting until marriage to have sex. This perceived hypocrisy will reflect poorly on the Guy campaign."

"Well, you heard it here first," the newscaster says, turning to the camera. "Remember, WCBF is your first source for election coverage!"

I hit the power button on the remote and lean back on the couch, not bothering to center my laptop so Hanna has a good view of me.

"Are you okay?" she asks.

"I . . ." What did I expect? That he'd be all torn up five months later? Did I think he'd be sitting around, lonely and miserable, wishing he'd given me a chance to explain? I couldn't even accept a date with my cute neighbor, and Sam's making sex tapes. "I'm fine. It's no big deal."

"The guy who broke your heart *is* a big deal, especially when he's on the national news. It's okay to be mad at him. Bad enough that he hasn't come crawling back to you—and he should have—but for you to find out this way . . ."

"Hanna, I'm gonna go."

"I love you, sis."

"I love you too." I close my laptop before she can say more and before I can start crying. As soon as I'm safe from the camera, I take the envelope addressed to Sam from my purse, and I rip it in half.

CHAPTER THREE

Sam

I DON'T MEAN TO LOOK. Not at first. But my gaze catches on the screen of Connor's phone, and I see that telltale red hair. "No . . ." I scroll down the screen to see picture after private picture. "This can't be . . ."

"It is."

Sabrina Guy stands at the edge of my living room, hands tucked into the pockets of her black dress pants. Behind her is a short blond woman in wire-rimmed glasses and a black suit. If I hadn't been so focused on my own self-pity, I may have noticed before now that Connor wasn't alone.

"May I?" Sabrina asks, motioning to the couch across from me.

"Sure. Why the hell not?"

Sabrina and her blond companion settle onto the couch. I rub the back of my neck. I feel like a hundred pounds of tension are tied up right in that spot. "Where'd the pictures come from?" I ask Sabrina. "I don't remember pictures."

"They aren't pictures. They're still frames from a video."

Oh, fuck. Yeah, I remember that. She wanted to see herself with me like that—bound, at my mercy. The camera was a thrill at the time—for both of us. But fuck. "So it's over? Everyone knows?"

The blonde reaches across the coffee table and offers her hand. "I'm Erin McDaniel, Governor Guy's campaign manager."

Sabrina flashes an apologetic smile. "It's okay," she says slowly as she narrows her gaze on me. "I told Erin the truth."

"The *truth?*" I shake my head. Maybe I've had more to drink than I thought.

"And Connor knows too," she says. "Everyone knows that's you and me in the video."

I lean back in my chair and stare at Sabrina.

"It's unfortunate the video was leaked to the press," Erin says. "And as much as I'd like to go back in time and talk you out of bringing a camera into the bedroom, what's done is done. The video is out there. Now we need to do damage control. Christine's more conservative supporters are already beginning to back away."

I turn to Sabrina. "How drunk am I? Because I thought I knew a little bit about politics, but I can't figure out for the life of me what my sex life has to do with the presidential election. It shouldn't matter."

"*You* know that," Sabrina says. "*I* know that. But this is America—land of the free, home of the puritanical."

I lean forward, elbows on my knees, and rub my temples. "Can't we stop them from airing this?"

"I'm sorry," Sabrina says softly. "The best we can do now is . . ." She looks away, something ticking in her jaw as she studies the opposite wall. "We just have to make the best of a bad situation. We admit we've been having a secret affair and that I'm a giant hypocrite about premarital sex."

"Sabrina—"

She shakes her head. "It would help my mother a lot—it would help *me*—if you'd be willing to say this isn't just sex. That we've been seriously involved for months."

"You don't think people will question why we haven't been seen together?"

Erin clears her throat. "You say you didn't want your relationship to look like a political move, so you were keeping it quiet."

Sabrina reaches across the coffee table and takes my hand in hers. Her fingers are long and slim and feel cold under the hot palm of my hand. "We have to do this."

Just when I thought my life couldn't get any more fucked up. "How did the tape get leaked?" I ask. We should have destroyed it. Or never made it to begin with.

"We don't know," Erin says. "We have people looking into it, but right now we need to focus on damage control."

"It could be worse," Sabrina says.

Yeah, no shit.

I pull my hand from hers and scroll through the images on Connor's phone again. I forgot we even used the camera. It only happened once—one night when she whispered the fantasy in my ear. But once is all it takes.

As much as I hate to be involved in any kind of political maneuvering, I don't want this ruining Christine's chance at the White House.

"Okay," I say, looking at Sabrina. "We'll make the best of it."

Erin's shoulders sag. "Fabulous. We'll get to work on the story right away. America might be a little squeamish about bondage, but they love a love story, and hey, that *Fifty Shades* book did great, right? This can work in our favor if we spin it right. We'll release a statement tomorrow and get you on the morning show circuit for next week. We'll want you by Sabrina's side for campaign stops and we can leak to the press where you'll be on a couple of dates before—"

"Wait," I say. "Stop. I said I'll tell the press we're involved. I never agreed to carrying on some elaborate charade."

"Right," Erin says. "Here's the thing. I don't do halfway. That's why I'm good at my job. Halfway will only get Governor Guy halfway to the White House, in which case we should just quit now and let America think Sabrina is a dominatrix with loose morals."

"Submissive," I mutter.

"If we're going to do this," Erin says, ignoring me, "we need to do it right. America will think it's creepy that you two like kinky sex. Spin that into a secret love affair, and suddenly the country is on your side. We can make this work if we proceed with a plan. Can we count on you?"

It's like the beginning of a nightmare, only the one I was already living was much worse. "I don't want—"

"It doesn't have to be all that," Sabrina says. "Let's keep it simple. One step at a time. I'm hosting a fundraiser in Indianapolis Saturday night. It would mean a lot if you'd show up, get some face time next to me, maybe make a statement to a journalist or two. If you decide you'd be willing to help us more after that, great, but right now that's all I'm asking. One night."

Liz

It turns out the water in my shower doesn't get hot enough to wash the image of Sam and Sabrina out of my mind. I know because I tried.

I step out of the shower, dry myself off, and pull on my pajamas. When I go back out to my living room, Hanna is on my couch and the twins are sitting at her feet, long strands of drool streaming from their mouths as they chew on identical sets of toy keys.

"What are you doing here?" I ask her. "It's after nine. Don't the girls need to be in bed?"

She hops up and steps over the girls to wrap me in a hug. "Sophie and Josie wanted to visit Aunt Lizzy."

I grin at my nieces. They aren't identical. Sophie has dark curls, and Josie's hair is more of a dark blond. Frequently, people lament that the girls aren't identical, but Hanna and I, being fraternal twins, love it.

I scoop Sophie off the floor and bury my nose in her downy hair. She smells like strawberry shampoo, and half my tension falls away by the simple magic of inhaling her scent.

"Did you call him?" Hanna asks.

"You don't beat around the bush, do you?"

Shrugging, she takes her spot on the couch and pulls Josie into her lap. Hanna has always been stunning, but motherhood has given her an ethereal beauty. Or maybe it's just the peace that comes with settling down with the love of your life.

"No," I say. "And I'm not going to."

"You should."

I shake my head. "It hurts too much, imagining him moving on when I'm still trying to figure out how to get through the day knowing . . ." I squeeze my eyes shut and don't say any more. I can't stand how melodramatic I sound, like the emo teens who volunteer at headquarters.

"Are you sure you don't want to tell him how you feel?" She pulls a burp cloth from her purse and reaches

28

around Josie to wipe up Sophie's spittle stream. "Maybe if he knew you still loved him—"

"Hanna, it's not that simple." I duck my head and take another hit of my niece's hair. They should bottle this scent and call it *Serenity*. "Anyway, how I feel is irrelevant. He doesn't love me anymore. He obviously loves her now." And, damn, that was quick.

Hanna snorts. "Don't be naive. There's a difference between love and sex."

"Hey, Liz, do you know your—oh, hi."

Hanna and I both look toward the front of my apartment to see George leaning on the doorframe.

"I saw your door open and was just making sure everything's okay. I didn't mean to interrupt."

"You're not interrupting anything," I say.

"Sorry," Hanna says. "I must not have gotten it shut all the way when I came in."

"Come on in and meet my twin sister," I tell him. "Hanna, this is my neighbor, George. George, this is Hanna."

Hanna cuts her eyes to me, and thanks to that whole twin-brain thing, I know exactly what she's thinking. Something along the lines of "George is hot." Which is true. But probably also something like, "You should fuck George," which is just a bad idea.

She grins at him and extends her hand from the couch. "Pleasure to meet you."

"Likewise." He walks over to shake her hand, then squats to look at the babies. "Are these beauties yours?"

"Sophie and Josie," I say, "meet your Aunt Lizzy's neighbor, George."

Sophie grabs a fistful of his hair in greeting.

"Ouch! I'm sorry." I untangle the baby's fist from his hair. I know from experience how much that hurts.

George only chuckles. "I have a couple of nieces and nephews myself. Not the first time this mop's been tugged on."

"Aw," Hanna says. "I bet you're great with them." She gives me an I-told-you-so cocked brow.

"I'll get out of your way," he says. "Hanna, it's nice to meet you and your girls. Want me to pull the door closed on my way out?"

"Please," I say.

"Good to meet you too," Hanna says, only barely keeping the glee out of her voice.

Halfway out the door, George stops and turns to look at me. "You're even more gorgeous with a baby in your arms, Liz."

Thank God he pulls the door shut after that, but there's little chance he doesn't hear Hanna's squeal from the other side.

"Oh. My. God," she whispers. "He's so into you."

"I know," I mutter, avoiding her gaze.

"And he's hot."

"I know," I repeat.

"You should ask him out. That's just what you need, you know. I'm guessing a few hours in bed with that hunk of man meat would cheer up any girl. Sam's dirty sex tape be damned."

"Hanna!"

She laughs, unashamed. "What? I'm married, not blind. He's hot. And my God, you clearly didn't see the way he was looking at you, because if you had, you'd be following him back to his apartment right now instead of sitting here talking to me."

"He already asked me out, and I declined."

Hanna blinks at me. "Who are you, and what did you do with my sister?"

"I'm not ready yet."

Her face softens. "Oh, Liz. I really wish you'd talk to Sam. Will told Cally that he's a mess. He misses you."

"He's with Sabrina Guy."

"There's no way he's serious about that girl," she says. "Who knows how old that video is?"

I grimace. Somehow, that doesn't make me feel any better. "Even if he weren't serious about her, we haven't exactly built a foundation for happily-ever-after. You know what his last words to me were? He said, 'I can't even look at you.' I screwed up. I should have told him about River the *second* I realized it wasn't Sam."

"Everyone screws up," she says. "Look at me. You made a mistake, but that doesn't make what happened your fault."

I'm so sick of thinking about it, and my body is so tense while thinking about it that I have to remind myself to breathe. "You know what I've realized? It wouldn't have mattered. I had dirty and completely inappropriate online conversations with his *father*." Just saying the words makes my stomach crawl up into my throat. I exhale slowly. "It doesn't matter if that came out sooner or later. We were doomed before we began."

She nods thoughtfully. "You know what Nate told me? Do you remember that night after I got out of the hospital? We went to Asher's house and we didn't know about my history with Nate yet, and you were intent on seducing him."

I shudder. "I don't exactly think of my brother-in-law that way anymore, but thanks for the reminder."

"That's not my point. Nate said Sam walked up to him that night and pointed you out and told Nate you were his. When you thought Sam was all about the hookup, he was already looking for more from you."

My stomach does a happy flip at that story, but the misplaced joy hurts more than soothes. It doesn't matter how Sam felt two years ago. "What's your point?"

"You've underestimated Sam from the beginning. Be careful you're not doing that now."

Am I underestimating him? Or is Hanna overestimating his feelings for me?

CHAPTER FOUR

Sam

IT WASN'T THAT HARD to find out which of Asia's stories were true and which were lies.

I tracked her down after Christmas—after Liz left and I was desperate to think about anything but the things she said to my father, the things he wrote to her. Instead of facing my feelings about Liz, I asked Asia to tell me the truth. She wouldn't. More lies. More contradictions. More smoke and mirrors.

But it wasn't that hard to dig up the truth. She delivered a baby about seven months after she made me believe she'd had an abortion. It wasn't that hard to track down the family who adopted the child and confirm the little girl was being raised by a family who truly loved her.

What's hard is not knowing if she's really mine. What's hard is believing Connor—and therefore my father—had something to do with taking the choice away from me.

I've been sitting here for an hour, parked in front of the little house in a suburb west of Indianapolis. I don't know what I'm doing here. I have no desire to take my child from them. She's a toddler now, and they're all she's ever known. Sure, I could start some big court battle. But even if I thought that was the best thing for her—and I don't—any chance I had of winning her back went down the drain when that video surfaced.

But here I am, sitting in a cold car in the dark as the moon climbs in the sky and blankets the house and yard in soft light. The house went dark hours ago. They put the baby down around seven thirty each night, then her parents watch some TV and cuddle on the couch, a snapshot from an ideal life I'll never have.

I don't often torture myself by watching their perfect little life. But I've had a shitty day—a shitty five months—and if I want to wallow in self-pity for a few fucking hours, I'm going to.

My phone rings. I see Max's name on the display and send the call to voicemail. He's worried about me. After I walked in on my dad and Liz in his office on Christmas day, I lost it there for a while.

She left me. Lizzy left me. She took that job with the governor and moved to Indianapolis. We both knew she was running away. What did I expect? I was so fucking pissed. No. I was *hurt*. I'd given her my heart. I trusted her.

It took a while, but eventually I was able to see that Liz did nothing wrong. She thought I was Riverrat, and when she had reason to believe I wasn't, she stopped their daily exchanges.

So she left me, and I let her. I couldn't even look at her. Her face was a reminder of my parents' sham of a marriage. She played a part in breaking my mom's heart again. The whole mess made me truly examine, for the first time in my life, what a fucking phony my father is. I thought it was easier to let her go than to deal with that. I was wrong.

And now *I'm* the phony with the pretend relationship and the lies.

I've imagined this little girl tracking me down one day. Maybe when she's in college and wants to know her roots. I'll wait until she comes to me, but if I let this scandal blow up, I may look like a freak she never wants to meet. I agreed to help, but not just for the sake of Christine's campaign. I did it for the little girl who might share my blood.

Liz

"She's hot," the phone bank volunteer says. "I mean, what guy *wouldn't* do that with her if she's game for it?"

"Yeah." I take a deep breath and try to figure out the best way to explain—*again*—how he's supposed to handle potential voters' concerns about the governor's daughter's sex life. I'm not sure why we're trusting this task to a man whose skinny jeans are tight enough to threaten the future of his family tree. "You see, voters don't need to know whether or not you're attracted to Sabrina. What they need is reassurance that Governor Guy condemns the release of that very private video of her daughter and that though she would have preferred her daughter wait until marriage to have sex, she supports Sabrina in all aspects of her life. Sabrina is her own person and she makes her own decisions."

"What does her mom even have to do with her sex life, am I right?" Mr. Hipster says.

"You're right." I force a smile. I want to love this job, but I'd be lying if I said it was anything like what I expected. Essentially, I'm a grunt worker.

During the short time I worked for Mr. Bradshaw, I was able to write speeches and organize events. I was one of a small number of cogs in the very important wheel of his campaign. Here, for Governor Guy's campaign, I'm one of dozens of staffers. Some days, the most important thing I do is fetch coffee for her campaign manager. That's right. I'm not important enough to fetch the *candidate's* coffee, but Erin McDaniel takes her coffee black.

It's not that I don't like my job. There's something

thrilling and energizing about being here with a woman who plans to change the world. I used to idolize Governor Guy, but now that I work for her, she's not just some symbol of feminine strength, a political power. She's become real to me, and I *respect* her.

But today, the job just sucks. All day long, I've been training volunteers how to "frame" the story of Sam and Sabrina's kinky sex tape. I spent the first half of the day nauseated, but at this point, I'm just numb.

"I've got this, Liz," the hipster promises. "Don't sweat it."

When he picks up his phone and gets back to work, Grace, one of my fellow staffers, sidles up to me and hands me a hot cup of coffee.

Grace is a year younger than me but with twice the spunk. She has an eyebrow ring and a penchant for wearing bright red lipstick. She wears her short black hair spiked half the time and under a do-rag the other half.

"I don't know about you," she says between sips of coffee, "but I'll be glad when Sabrina makes a statement. Once she lets the world know she's in love and they can fuck themselves and their puritanical obsession with and condemnation of kinky sex, *our* jobs will be a lot easier."

I shake my head. "I don't think she's going to say Americans can fuck themselves."

"No." She gives a reluctant grunt. "I guess not. But *damn*, weren't those pictures hot? I mean, that guy can tie me up any day of the week."

Of course, it's right as Grace says the bit about being

tied up that the constant hum of conversation in the phone room goes quiet. Everyone turns to her, and she grins and waggles her eyebrows.

When the workers get back to their conversations, she turns to me. "Hey, I forgot to tell you—a family canceled for Sabrina's event downtown tomorrow night. Probably because of that tape, but they made up some excuse. Anyway, you know how Ms. Guy feels about empty seats. Sabrina's asking staff to fill in. Can you be there?"

I shrug. I've gone to any number of fundraisers, rallies, and black-tie affairs since I moved up here after Christmas. The only plans I had for tomorrow were to bandage my broken heart with a pint of Ben & Jerry's. This will give me a better excuse to get out of girls' night in New Hope. "Yeah. Of course."

"Awesome! We'll sit together. Oh, and be warned, sexy McBondage is going to be there with Guy's daughter."

Well, fuck.

She smacks her lips. "Think they have one of those open relationships?"

"I somehow doubt it."

"Well, whatever. See you tomorrow night. Wear something hot. Maybe we can talk him into a threesome if he ever leaves Sabitchna."

I adore Grace, but sometimes I want to take her into a corner and tell her she doesn't have to try so hard. She's not the only staffer who's dubbed Sabrina *Sabitchna,* but Grace doesn't dislike Sabrina as much as she likes calling her names for shock value. I'm not sure Sabrina actually deserves the title. She can be a little abrasive, true, but she knows what she's doing.

"I'm sorry to break it to you," I say, "but I'm not interested in a threesome with Sam Bradshaw."

She gives a heavy sigh. "Okay, well, since *that* plan is shot to hell, feel free to bring a date."

"I'm sure I'll be all by my lonesome, but thanks."

I spend the rest of my workday under a shroud of nervous anxiety about the possibility of seeing Sam, and by the time I'm driving back to my apartment, I'm a wreck. Traffic isn't too bad, but I still feel as if I'm winding tighter with every block.

"It's just for work," I remind myself.

When I reach my floor, George is locking his door. We cross paths a lot and he's always dressed well, but he looks especially nice tonight in an Oxford shirt and a tie.

"Hot date?" I ask.

He grins. "That depends. Are you available?"

I shake my head and wave away his question. "Have fun."

"Will do. Hey, a guy was here looking for you this morning."

My chest feels heavy and I turn around slowly. "Who was it? Are you sure he was looking for me?"

"Yeah. He wanted to talk to you about something important."

My heart's playing a game of cat and mouse in my chest, pulsing frantically forward and then slowing in fear. "Did he tell you his name?"

"No, but I recognized his face from the news." He

frowns, as if trying to figure out a puzzle. "How do you know Sam Bradshaw?"

Sam

Mom enters my office and closes the door behind her. My mom is low on my list of people I want to look in the eye the morning after my sex tape goes live.

"You didn't have to keep it a secret," she says. "You know your father and I would have been thrilled to know you were dating Sabrina."

I exhale slowly and rub the back of my neck. "I'm not interested in sharing anything about my love life with my father."

"Right. Well, I guess he earned that." She forces a smile. "I talked to Sabrina this morning. She called me, bless her heart. A mother shouldn't learn her son's secrets from the media, and she wanted me to hear the truth about your relationship from her."

The truth. Funny that Sabrina put it that way. I guess it's good practice. "Not sure what she could have said that hasn't already been shown to millions of people."

"I know you don't want to air more of your personal business, but I'm so glad you two are going public about your relationship."

"The only thing that matters is how a relationship

looks to the world. Isn't that right, Mom?" She flinches, and I feel like a dick. "That was low. I'm sorry. Dad's the one who screwed up. I don't mean to rub the past in your face." And I don't want to be involved in something that hurts her. Not again.

Mom hangs her head and exhales slowly, her petite shoulders folding in, as if she's been walking around carrying the weight of the world and she's worn out. When she lifts her head, she meets my eyes with a fire in her gaze I've never seen before. "You sit there and you judge me for staying with your father, you judge your father for falling for the girl you wanted, but you have no idea what it's like to be married to the same person for thirty years. Marriage isn't one long honeymoon. Your father and I do love each other. It's just different than it used to be. I don't expect you to understand. But I do expect you to respect me as your mother enough not to question my decision to stay with him."

"I didn't say a word," I say.

"Exactly. You don't say anything. You avoid me. You avoid your father. You treat Della's husband like he's the help. You're angry at the world." She takes a breath and softens her voice. "You liked the girl. I understand that. But don't make her out to be some saint in this. You read the things she wrote to him. You saw the pictures she sent. Any man would have fallen for that. Any man would have lost his way for a minute. Don't be so angry. She's not who you think, and your future with her wouldn't have been this bright and shiny thing you imagine. I'm *grateful* it worked out this way."

I ball my fists but don't reply. Liz *is* good. She's so good she hasn't tried to talk to me, or anyone in my family, since I sent her away.

"Sabrina said you two really started getting close when you were broken up over Liz, and if that's what it took to get you with someone good, I'm glad."

Leave it to Sabrina to put all the pieces together into a story even my mom can find romantic. I'm tempted to tell my mom not to start planning our wedding, but I don't want to risk her asking questions about me and Sabrina that I can't answer.

"You'll understand someday," Mom says. "Someday, you'll be able to look back and see that this all worked out for the best."

CHAPTER
FIVE

Liz

"DEFINITELY A RED ONE," Cally says, tossing a purple contender to the floor.

"Agreed," Maggie says. "She looks too fuckable in red to wear anything else." She flips through the dresses hanging from the shower in her and Asher's massive master bathroom.

Last night, I called Hanna to tell her a) I would be seeing Sam at a black-tie event tomorrow, and b) he showed up at my apartment. She decided I had to come to New Hope and let them help me get ready for the event.

When I arrived at Maggie's this morning, Krystal, Hanna, Cally, and Nix all met me at the door, like my own team of personal stylists. I've been here for twenty minutes and have learned that the girls have many opinions on what I should be wearing and how I should look. I've also learned that the girls all think Sabrina is "the rebound booty call" and that Sam's not serious about her.

"That one!" Hanna shouts from behind me. She jumps up and down and claps her hands. "Yes, that one!"

Maggie holds up the red halter dress. "This one's hot. I wore it to the AMAs, and it's too stupid expensive not to be worn again."

"I remember," Hanna says. "It's perfect for Liz tonight."

Krystal folds her arms. "How is it that my sisters have such exciting lives they get to sit with their rocker boyfriends at the American Music Awards when the biggest excitement of my week is ordering a pizza?"

Krystal is my oldest sister. There are five of us, and she's always been an outsider. As twins, of course Hanna and I are BFFs. Then Maggie is only a year younger than us, so we've always been close to her too. But then there are Krystal and Abby—the oldest and the youngest—and they always seem to be on the outside. Since Krystal moved back to New Hope from Florida, she's been spending more time with our growing group. It's been nice.

"You're singing my song, girl," Nix says.

Krystal and Nix high-five, then Krystal turns to me. "I like the dress, but I want to see it on you."

I don't bother protesting when the girls work

together to dress me. Maggie's AMA dress is cut low in the back. It's fitted around my hips and ass and hits mid-thigh, showing off my legs.

Krystal puts a finger to her lips. "I'm not sure it's slutty enough."

"I'm going for *work*," I remind her, "not to start hooking."

"Here." Maggie hands me a pair of matching red stilettos.

I step into them, and everyone goes quiet. "What?" I ask, turning toward the mirror.

"Totally fuckable," Maggie says. "Sam's an idiot if he thinks he's going to be happier with someone else."

I bite my lip. I can't imagine the damage my mistakes with River did to his family. "You know, his parents have always wanted him to be with Sabrina. Maybe that's what he needs to do to bring his family back together."

"Why is it his job to fix his family?" Nix asks.

Hanna is studying me, and I know if she had her way, it would be just the two of us. She'd have me crying and spilling my guts to her in no time.

"So fill me in on the latest gossip," I say, mostly so Hanna will stop looking at me like that. "What have I missed?"

"Not much," Krystal says. "Everyone in town seems so excited that Mr. Bradshaw is leading in the polls and, by all appearances, will be the next governor. Though, between you, me, and the wall, I don't think his speeches are as good now that you're not writing them."

God bless sisters and the things they say to boost our egos. Too bad I know better. "I wasn't a speechwriter for him for very long."

"His best speeches were the ones you wrote," Hanna says. "And he still uses lines from them."

I'm not sure if the first part is true. It's not like I have real skill. He only hired me because he knew I was Tink24. As foolish as it is, that's one of the things that hurts the most. I hate being stupid. Being able to write speeches for Travis Bradshaw's gubernatorial campaign made me feel special and smart and talented, but it turned out I wasn't any of those things. I was just a stupid girl who had dirty conversations with him online, and he hired me so I'd be closer to him.

"It's true," Cally says. "The speeches you wrote had something special about them. They felt more, I don't know, sincere? But we're happy to support you wherever you want to be and whatever you want to do."

"It's not like she could keep working for him," Maggie says. She shudders and wrinkles her nose. "Riverrat. More like *rat bastard.*"

"He's such a fucking prick," I mutter.

"Amen," Maggie says.

"A dirty old man," Hanna says. "Hiring you, like you were going to fuck him in his office or something."

The girls all know about what happened. I didn't take Bradshaw's stupid hush money, and I don't like keeping things from them. The secret made me feel so dirty, I had to tell it, if only in the hopes of distancing myself from it.

"Are Sam's parents okay?" I ask. "How's their

marriage?" I may hate Mr. Bradshaw, but Mrs. Bradshaw was nothing but welcoming to me. I'm sure she regrets that now. I don't think I could look her in the eye again if I had to.

Maggie flashes me a sympathetic look. "They're still smiling for the cameras. What you need to understand is that if their marriage falls apart, it isn't about you. It's about *him*. He knew he was married. You didn't. He knew you were way too young for him. You didn't. He misled you in the worst way."

"No one blames you," Hanna says.

I press my hand to my angry stomach. Most days it feels like there's a war being fought in there. "Yes, they do. And I *was* the 'other woman,' so maybe they should."

Maggie takes my shoulders and turns me to face her. Her green eyes are intense, her jaw set in a hard line. "Don't you dare. This is not on you."

"Right. Of course not." Those words aren't convincing anyone. Then, because I can't help myself, I ask, "How is he?"

"Sam?" Krystal says. "He's a train wreck." When everyone turns to her, she shrugs. "What? We work out at the same health club. I see him all the time. He's a mess. This Sabrina must really like the fixer-uppers."

Hanna winces. "That's just probably not what Liz wants to hear right now."

Krystal snorts. "Why not? You know, I once called off my wedding to a guy I was madly in love with. I only *wished* he'd be beside himself with grief." She looks to Cally. "Glad he wasn't, of course. You're way better for him than I ever was."

"Thanks," Cally says, shifting awkwardly.

Krystal turns back to me. "My point is, Sam would be fine if he didn't miss you so much. That boy has it bad for you. I don't care what the world thinks about him and Sabrina Guy. She's the rebound. You're the real deal."

"Maybe he should have called her," Nix says. "Regardless of how he feels now, he behaved like an ass. At the very least, he should have touched base with her when his sex tape went public."

Hanna cuts her eyes to me, but she keeps her mouth shut.

"He came to my place yesterday," I say so the other girls know why Hanna's looking at me like that.

"Oh," says Nix. "Wow. How did that go? Was it too little, too late?"

"I wasn't there." I shrug. "I don't think he was planning to beg me to take him back or anything."

"But maybe he was," Hanna says. In Hanna's mind, the glass isn't half full; it's overflowing.

I shake my head. "Intentionally or not, I had an affair with his father, who is still married to his mother. It's safe to say my first Christmas with that family was also my last."

"You need to talk to him before you make any more assumptions," Hanna says.

Maggie nods. "I actually agree."

With a sigh, I study myself in the mirror and imagine Sam spotting me while I'm wearing this dress. He loved me once, right? Can that really be gone?

I wish I still believed that love could conquer all, but any remnant of that childish notion was washed away when I saw the way Sam looked at me on Christmas Day.

I smooth the dress into place and nod. "I'll do something with my hair and put on a little makeup and be good to go."

"You need one more thing," Krystal says.

"What's that?" I ask.

"A date."

Sam

I've always been a "rip off the Band-Aid" kind of guy. None of that "tiny bit at a time" pussy shit. Just do it.

Which is why I'm at the gym early Saturday morning to work out with my best friends, despite knowing that I haven't seen or spoken with them since the pictures came out.

I've been here twenty minutes, and neither Max nor Will has mentioned it. *Assholes.*

I step behind the bench press to spot Will. "So you guys probably know I'm with Sabrina Guy now."

"Yeah," Max says, clearing his throat as he sits in front of the leg press. "We, um, saw that."

"And what I would give to unsee it," Will mutters as

he pushes up the bar.

"Shut the fuck up, both of you."

"And here we thought you hadn't left the house for anything but work and the gym since Liz left town," Will says. He settles the bar back onto the rack and sits up, catching his breath. "Clearly, we were mistaken."

No, they weren't. Not really. But if I want my secrets to remain my own, I need to start here.

"So," Max says, "you're serious about her? The governor's daughter—what's her name? Katrina?"

"Sabrina. And, yeah, um, I guess."

"Watch that enthusiasm, dude," Will says. "She might think you want it too much."

"Why haven't we met this Sabrina?" Max asks.

I groan. "She's busy."

"Yeah," Will says. "Looks like she's been pretty *tied up.*" He dodges when he sees my fist coming for his shoulder. "Sorry. I couldn't resist."

"*Try,*" I growl.

Max stands and cocks his head at me. "You'd tell us if you were in trouble or something, right?"

"I'm fine. I'm just not into all this spotlight crap. And now that everyone . . ." *Fuck.* I hate lying to my best friends. But if I tell them the truth, they'll tell their wives, and then it'll get back to Liz. Hell, maybe I want that. Maybe I want Liz to know I'm not attached to anyone.

But what's the point?

"Now that everyone what?" Max asks.

I sigh. "Now that everyone knows about Sabrina and me, tonight I have to go to this bullshit fundraiser in

Indy. As if I don't have enough of that crap with my father."

"Oh, yeah," Will says. "Cally said something about that this morning. She was going over to Maggie's with some dresses to help find something for Liz to wear. It's at the reception center next to the Conrad, right?"

I stiffen. "Liz is going?"

Max arches an eyebrow at Will, who grimaces. "Sorry."

I look at Max. "Why is he apologizing?"

"Because you get butt-sore every time someone brings up Liz. Which is awfully strange for a guy who's telling the world—and his best friends—that he's serious about another woman."

CHAPTER SIX

Liz

I'M FULLY CAPABLE of doing my own hair and makeup, but I let them fuss over me, and it felt good. My hair's off my neck in a twist with only several loose curls free at the nape of my neck, and I'm wearing a pair of Mom's diamond studs. But my favorite part of my whole getup is the red lipstick. It makes me feel sexy, bold, and confident. Definitely not like the heartbroken girl desperate to make her ex's jaw drop.

"You look like you're going somewhere special tonight."

I turn to see George and smile. "Well, not in this." Not wanting to wrinkle the dress, I drove home in jeans, a button-up shirt, and my fancy makeup. "I have a dress that's much more flattering."

He slides his gaze down my body. "Any more flattering and guys are going to trip over themselves to get to you."

My cheeks warm. *Just do it.* "Do you know our neighbor, Mrs. Louise?"

"She brings me meals on a regular basis," he says.

"Me too. But in addition to worrying that I don't eat enough, she worries I don't date enough."

"You too, huh?" He grins, then cocks his head after pausing a beat. "Does this mean you're reconsidering my offer?"

"Any chance you're free tonight?"

* * *

"If I went for girls, I would totally take you to the bathroom and have you do me against the wall," Grace says when I walk up to our table.

"Grace!" I screech.

Beside me, George grins. "I'd be happy to guard the door. From the inside, of course. Better security that way."

"You're so selfless," I mutter.

"That's what all my dates say."

"Who's the hottie?" Grace asks.

"George, this is my co-worker, Grace. Grace, meet George."

He takes her hand, but gives me a sideways glance

when Grace holds on too long and molests him with her eyes.

"I approve," she says with a nod. "Let me get you two a drink. It's an open bar. Wine for the lady, beer for the man?" She saunters off without waiting for our reply.

George pulls out my chair for me, then takes the spot beside mine. The ballroom is a veritable who's who of Indiana money and politics. Everyone looks amazing, decked out in sleek formal gowns and custom-cut tuxedos.

When Grace returns, she settles a large glass of red wine in front of me and a pint in front of George before taking the free seat beside me.

"Oh my God." She points across the room. "Look, it's Mr. Bradshaw. Check him out. Now I see where his son gets his good looks."

I would rather eat week-old gas station sushi than check out Mr. Bradshaw, but I force a smile and slide a cursory glance in his direction. "Not my type."

I scan the room and my eyes snag on Sam and Sabrina at a table near the stage. They're talking to an Indiana senator, big smiles on both their faces. Sabrina leans into Sam, and he keeps his arm wrapped around her shoulders in a way that's almost more brotherly than intimate.

In your dreams, I remind myself. But ever since the video was leaked, something's been niggling at me. Maybe it's just that he didn't seem interested in her at all last winter, but I feel as if there's more. My gut tells me I'm missing something.

Too bad the last year has cost me all the confidence I have in my gut. I should know by now that where other people have a gut, I have wishful thinking. Why else would I have been *so sure* Sam was River?

"Earth to Liz," Grace says. "Try not to be so obvious with the man-lust, 'kay? You might hurt your date's feelings."

I look to George, who's watching me with eyes that look more worried than jealous.

"Sorry," I say.

He shakes his head. "You never did tell me how you knew him."

I paste on a smile. "I told you he's an old friend."

He takes the wine from in front of me and drains half of it. "Right."

"Did I tell you about the time I dated twin brothers at the same time?" Grace asks.

George and I let Grace entertain us with her wild stories through dinner. I manage a few bites, but my heart's not in it tonight. After the plates are cleared and dessert is served, Sabrina gets on stage, and everyone quiets for her speech.

"You all probably feel as if you've been seeing too much of me lately," she begins, and the crowd laughs.

George is watching me, so I force a smile and give Sabrina my attention. After apologizing that her private life has detracted from her mother's campaign, she introduces Sam, who stands at their table and lifts a hand in greeting to the crowd.

"I love that guy," she says with a grin. "Best thing that ever happened to me."

He winks at her. When my heart is all but torn from my chest, she finally begins talking about her mom's vision for her presidency, and I breathe again.

Sabrina finishes her speech and invites everyone to the dance floor. As she leaves the stage, Sam takes her hand and leads her to the dance floor, and I feel like they have my heart out there with them, right under their feet, and I'm just sitting here hollow inside.

"Go on, you two," Grace says. "The campaign needs you to go out there and look beautiful."

"May I have a dance?" George asks.

I don't want to be that close to America's sweethearts over there, but I *am* the one who asked George to come with me tonight. "That would be nice."

He offers his hand and we make our way to the dance floor.

Sam and Sabrina are already dancing. They look beautiful together. They're on the opposite side of the dance floor, and she smiles up at him as he leads her. Every so often she leans her head against his chest, and the gesture is so intimate that something inside of me cracks at the sight.

"Have I mentioned how beautiful you look tonight?" George whispers in my ear.

I startle and tear my eyes away from the couple of the night so I can look at my date. "Thank you. You look handsome too."

He cocks a brow. "Well, thanks. I wasn't aware you'd actually looked at anyone but him."

I follow his gaze back to Sam and force a laugh. "Am I staring? After that video, I think everyone is curious about those two. I hope I'm not being rude, but I have a weakness for gossip magazines."

He wrinkles his brow. "Yeah? I don't know you very well, but I wouldn't have pegged you for the gossip magazine type."

"Guilty pleasure."

"Liz, you don't look at him like you're curious. You look at him like you're heartbroken."

My stomach flutters nervously. "Don't be silly."

His arms are warm and sure as they fold me into his chest. A year ago, before I fell hard for Sam, a guy like George was exactly what I thought I wanted—nice, successful, attractive. But tonight my heart belongs to someone else.

Maybe it did a year ago, too. Maybe that's why I could never find anyone. I didn't want guys like George or even guys *like* Sam. I wanted Samuel Bradshaw, no exceptions, no substitutions, and I was too scared to admit it to myself.

"You're staring at him again," George says.

"Shit."

He pulls back to look me in the eye. "Listen, I know you're both from New Hope, and I know that you know his family. Add that to his visit to your apartment and the way you act when he's around, and I don't need to be Sherlock to guess he's the guy who broke your heart."

I duck my head into his chest. "It doesn't matter. We've both moved on."

"It appears he's moved on," he says, his hand sliding up to the exposed skin of my back. "But I've been living next door to you for five months, and you've been miserable. I think time stopped for you the day he broke your heart."

"That's dramatic." But my eyes are burning with tears, and I feel one escape and roll down my cheek. "Shit."

He holds the back of my head and cradles my face against his chest. "Don't let him see you cry. He's not worth it."

CHAPTER SEVEN

Sam

MY GUT TWISTS every time my gaze snags on Liz in that guy's arms. All night I've been asking myself why I didn't go to her sooner. Or call her. Anything.

Sure, I've been dealing with my own shit. In addition to finding out the woman I love had an online affair with my father, there was the whole Asia thing, and the baby, and the role Connor and my father may or may not have played in that mess. It's hard to figure out how to fix an impossible relationship when you're busy brooding over your fucked life.

My family's imploding, and when she left me it was

easier to blame her than it was to forgive her. Maybe that's still the easier path.

Yesterday, I looked up Liz and drove to her apartment on impulse. Just showed up as if she'd even want to see me, and as if I even knew what to say.

"Hey, I know I was a dick last time we talked, but I wanted to warn you that there's this video. Oh, right, you've already seen the highlight reel, like the rest of the world. Okay, so, I hope you're not hurt by this, but then again, I hope you are because that would mean you still give two fucks."

Right, so she didn't exactly miss out on my most eloquent speech by being at work.

"Try looking at me," Sabrina says. "Pretend she's not here."

I smile down at my date as if I'm the happiest asshole in the world. "Who?"

"Seriously?" She rolls her eyes and shakes her head. "What's up with you two, anyway? You were all touchy at your father's fundraiser before Christmas. What happened?"

I spot a journalist out of the corner of my eye and skim a kiss over Sabrina's shoulder. I hope we don't have to do much of this shit. The charade is going to get really old, really fast. I wait until he's snapped a few pictures before I continue our conversation.

"Things fell apart." Unwillingly, my eyes seek out Liz and her date again. They're on the other side of the dance floor, and she's curled into his chest as if the world is bad and dangerous and he is her safe place. Which fucking pisses me off. *I'm* supposed to be her safe place. Who is he, anyway? Are they serious? *Serious enough that she took him to a work event and that she snuggles into his chest while she dances with him.*

"I'll tell you what," Sabrina says. She slides her hand into my hair and turns my head just slightly so I'm looking at her instead of across the dance floor. "You get through this with me, and I'll help you put things back together with Blondie." She frowns. "If that's what you want, that is."

"I . . ." I don't know what I want. To be someone else. To not be my father's son. To start over. I shake my head. "As much as I respect the infinite strings you pull in all walks of life, Sabrina, I don't think my relationship with Liz is something you can fix."

"You've been carrying a torch for her for a long time. Sometimes, we're only hurting ourselves by not letting go." She gives me a sad smile that tells me she's not just talking about Liz. She's talking about her feelings for me.

Guilt shames me into keeping my eyes off Liz and on Sabrina.

"Wasn't it this time last year that you told me you were holding out for her?" she asks. "That she was *the one* for you?"

The memory of that night cuts me. I was so determined to make Liz mine, and a few days later I opened the door to Connor's apartment to find Liz sleeping naked in his arms. I should have known we were doomed from the start. Maybe Sabrina's right.

SOMETHING REAL

* * *

One year ago . . .

"How have you been?" Sabrina asks. She gives me that timid little smile that makes me feel like an ass. I know she's had a crush on me since we were teenagers, but I can't very well tell her why I'm so dead-set against dating her.

"I'm good. Busy, but you know how it is."

"I do." She drops her gaze to the floor and bites her lip. "I have this silly dinner I have to go to this weekend for Mom. Is there any way I could talk you into going with me?"

"Sabrina?" I wait while her vulnerable eyes meet mine. "I'm kind of . . . involved with someone."

She frowns. "I know you're single, Sam. You can tell me the truth if you don't want to go with me."

"It's complicated." My gaze drifts across the bar and lands on Liz sitting in a booth with her sister, Maggie. "Let's just say I'm holding out for the right thing."

"Her?" Sabrina follows my gaze to Liz. "Really? So, what's the holdup? Does she have a boyfriend? Married? Venereal disease? What?"

My stomach twists. I haven't been with Liz since the night William and Cally got married. I'd all but given up on getting her to give me a chance, and then there she was the night of the wedding, offering herself to me like a gift and drawing me in all over again.

I haven't bothered dating anyone else since. She's all I want.

"She has a history with Connor, doesn't she?" Sabrina asks.

"I guess," I admit. "How did you know that?"

"Your sister found out about their hookup or whatever."

When Connor took Lizzy's virginity. *Bastard.* "Della wasn't even *with* Connor then."

Sabrina shrugs. "Doesn't matter. She found out, and now she hates her a little."

I don't care about Liz's history with Connor. Sure, I want to cut his dick off every time I think about that night, but I can hardly blame Liz. She was young, naive, and vulnerable.

The real thing keeping me from Liz is Liz herself. She doesn't take me seriously. She doesn't understand how much I want her. Or maybe she does, and the feeling isn't reciprocal.

"Well," Sabrina says, "good luck making it work."

I nod, but I can't take my eyes off Liz. "Thanks."

Liz
Present day . . .

"I'm sorry I made you cry," George says as we head back to our table. "I didn't mean to upset you."

He held me on the dance floor until my tears dried and I composed myself again. I doubt a single person even noticed I was upset. If anything, I probably looked a little *too* into my date.

"It's fine." We sit down, but the rest of the chairs at our table are empty. "I didn't realize I was so transparent, I guess."

Grace stumbles to our table and collapses into the chair next to me. Her dark eye makeup is smudged and her lipstick is fading. "Lizzy, Liz, Liz." She leans her head on my shoulder. "I am so completely trashed."

"I noticed." I smile and smooth her hair back from her face. "Do you need a ride home?"

She lifts her head an inch and grins without fully opening her eyes. "No. I got a room at the Conrad. My father is loaded, ya know, and he might be tight with his money but if it's for my"—she lifts her hands and makes air quotes—"'career,' he'll pay for anything I want. So, *ta-da*, room at the Conrad." She rolls her head back onto my shoulder. "But I didn't think I'd be staying in it alone. Who knew that there wouldn't be an assortment of single guys looking for an easy lay at this thing?"

"Even if there were," George says, "we wouldn't let you go back to your room with a stranger. Not in your condition."

"Party pooper."

"Come on." I slide my arm under hers. "Let's get you to bed."

George helps me get her up and over to the hotel. Grace is sober enough—thank God—that she remembers her room number. I find the keycard in her purse and we take her to her bed, and George turns around to give us some privacy as I help her into her PJs.

"See," Grace says, "even though I was totally hoping to spend the night with a hottie, I brought sleep clothes just in case. I'm *always prepared*." She laughs as if this is the funniest thing she's ever heard.

George helps me lead her to one of the two big beds, and we tuck her in.

"You need some water," George says. He leaves for the bathroom.

"Don't leave me, Liz," Grace mumbles. "Stay and tell me a story. Or snuggle with me. Or something. I promise I won't feel you up in your sleep." She giggles and points to George, who's returned with a glass of water. "I wouldn't make the same promise to *you*, though."

I look to George. "You mind if I keep her company tonight?"

"Promise to take pictures?"

"You can be our photographer, George," Grace says.

I shake my head. Grace is like one of those college girls who has been sheltered all her life, and tries too hard to be cool and edgy once she's out on her own. "Drink the water, Grace. I'll be back in a few minutes."

I grab the key off the nightstand, and George and I go out to the hall.

"You're sure you're okay with this?" I ask when the door is closed behind us.

"It's not a problem. You're a good friend. She

65

shouldn't be alone."

"Thank you. For understanding and for . . . everything else. I'm sorry tonight wasn't a better first date."

He arches a brow. "So this *was* a date. I wasn't sure."

"Sure it was."

"In that case . . ."

I know what he's doing before he does it. He gives me enough time to stop it, but I don't. I let him slide his hand behind my neck, and when he lowers his lips to mine, I kiss him like a girl should kiss a boy at the end of their first date.

His lips are warm and soft, and he keeps the kiss brief, but when he pulls back my stomach falls because Sam is behind him, by all appearances attempting to burn holes into George with the intensity of his glare alone.

George turns around to follow my gaze, but Sam punches his keycard into his door and disappears into his room.

"Well." George clears his throat. "At least you know the neighbors, right?"

I give a shaky smile.

"I hope we can try this again sometime, maybe *without* your ex staring lasers into my back."

I bite my lip, not wanting to commit to anything. "Maybe for now you and I could just be . . ." I am the worst. *The worst.*

George sighs. "It was always about him, wasn't it? I've been friend-zoned before. I can handle it."

"Do you hate me?"

"Nah." His gaze drifts to Sam's door. "Jury's still out on him, though. Good night, Liz."

CHAPTER EIGHT

Sam

I JUST WANT to get drunk and think about Liz. Liz smiling. Liz naked. Liz moaning. Liz screaming my name as I make her come.

Liz anywhere but cradled in another man's arms.

I pour myself two fingers of bourbon, but I sip when I want to guzzle. I'm hoping the buzz about the video will die down soon, but for now, I always have to be "on"—ready to smile for the cameras and lie to the world. Probably better not to be hungover.

There's a knock on the door, so soft I almost miss it. But it comes again, a little louder this time.

Security had better not have let one of those asshole journalists from downstairs up to my floor. I swear, those soul suckers would do anything to get a new detail to add to their nothing stories. I open the door without removing the chain and feel as if I've been punched in the gut when I see the woman on the other side.

Liz is worrying her lower lip between her teeth and watching down the hall. Is she looking for Sabrina or trying to make sure no one sees her coming to my room? My insides twist at the sight of her—an internal tug-of-war between conflicting emotions. I want to pull her into my room and kiss her until she can't see straight, touch her until she promises never to leave me again, and at the same time, I want to demand that she go back to her room because having her close makes me hope for things I can't have.

I remove the chain and tug her inside by the arm before closing the door behind her.

"No one saw me," she says, her eyes locked on the floor. "I made sure."

"*I* saw you," I growl. It's painful to be this close—to breathe her air, to smell her perfume. I never knew how much it could hurt to *want* and be denied.

She swallows and avoids my eyes. "Is she here?"

"What do you want, Liz?"

She lifts her head and stares at me. "Is she here?"

"Sabrina's on her way to meet her mom in South Dakota for a campaign stop."

Her gaze dips to my bare chest and back up. "I'm surprised they didn't ask you to go with them."

"They did. I declined." I sound like a fucking dickhead, and I make myself take two steps back so I don't do something equally dickish. Like kiss her until she melts in my arms and forgets about the other guy, until we both forget that this is hopeless.

"I'm sorry that video was leaked. You didn't deserve that invasion of your privacy."

She has red lipstick on, and it matches her shoes. Ever since I saw her tonight, I've been picturing her on her knees in nothing but those shoes, those red lips stretched around my cock. I can't help myself, and I skim my thumb over her bottom lip.

The second I touch her, she draws in a ragged breath. "You came to my apartment yesterday."

"I did."

"Why?"

I trail my thumb down her neck and over the red strap of her dress. "Probably for the same reason you came here tonight."

"To talk about Sabrina?"

"You knocked on my door in the middle of the night to talk about Sabrina?" I follow the strap down and graze my fingers across her cleavage. "Is this about her, or is it about you and me?"

"There is no you and me," she says. "We both know that."

"There's so much you and me, there's no air left when we share a room. There's *always* you and me."

"Even when you're making sex tapes with someone else?"

"And even when you're keeping warm in another

man's arms," I say. "Who is he?"

"A friend."

I slide a hand behind her head and take a fistful of her hair. "Are you fucking him?"

Her face goes hard. "What if I were?"

"I'd have to keep you here. Touch you. Tease you. Taste you until you begged me to fuck you against this wall. Then I'd drive so deep inside you that you'd remember *no one* can get you off like I do."

She drags in a breath and licks her lips. "He's a friend."

I grunt but soften my grip on her hair. "Have you told him that? Because the way he looked at you when you two danced, the way he held you, he wants to be a hell of a lot more than your friend. Then there was that kiss in the hall . . ." I cup her jaw in my palm and try to talk myself out of pressing my mouth to hers.

"This is none of your business," she says, but she leans into my touch and her eyes float closed.

"But my relationship with Sabrina is yours?"

"I'm worried about you," she says. "I worry you're trying to protect her by lying about the extent of your relationship, and I'm wondering how far you'll go to perpetuate it."

"You don't need to worry about me. But we both know that's not what brought you to my hotel room in that dress." I take a step closer, and she backs against the door. Our bodies are so close they're almost touching.

She lifts her chin in defiance, but her gaze slips to my lips. She wants my kiss as much as I want to give it to her. "I shouldn't have come."

"Are you sure about that? We want each other. That didn't change just because you left." Unable to resist anymore, I dip my head and press an open-mouthed kiss to her bare shoulder. Her skin is cool and smells like flowers. *Christ.* "Why'd you run away, Rowdy?"

"I . . . I didn't run."

"You ran away."

"I took an opportunity."

I trail my fingers down the side of her waist. "You were scared and you ran away. You're only here now because my relationship with Sabrina makes it safe."

"So you do have a relationship with her?" she asks quietly.

"I'm not interested in talking about her. I asked about *you*. Why you ran away before we had a chance. But fuck five months ago. Let's talk about right now." I find the hem of her skirt and take it into my fist. "Tell me what you *want*."

"I . . . I want . . ." She shakes her head and ducks under my arm, escaping my touch.

I grab her wrist and spin her around, pressing her against the wall as I step close again. When I press my lips to her neck, she doesn't try to escape again. Instead, her hands go to my waist and work their way up as she slowly unbuttons my shirt.

"Tell me you haven't missed this," I whisper against her ear.

Her lips part and her gaze dips to my mouth. "I can't."

"Tell me you want me to stop."

"I can't," she repeats.

"You can't stay?" I slide my hand under her skirt and she draws in a sharp breath. "Or you can't tell me to stop?"

Her only answer is to release the final button on my shirt and to give a slight shift of her hips toward my hand. She pushes my shirt from my shoulders, and I let it drop. Then I inch up her thigh, reveling in the feel of her soft skin under my fingertips. She wraps a hand around my biceps and her nails bite into the back of my arm as I cup her between her legs.

"You're already wet for me." I brush my fingertips over the center of her panties then slip my fingers under the damp fabric and stroke her clit.

My ears fill with the sounds of her uneven breathing, and I close my eyes for a second—but only a second, because I don't want to miss the pleasure on her face. She's beautiful every minute of every day, but when she's turned on, when I'm touching her . . .

She moans, a slight, desperate sound, one she was trying to hold back but couldn't contain. My dick swells painfully in the confines of my pants as I imagine keeping her here and making her moan all night.

"We shouldn't do this," she says. But she holds me close. "God, that feels so good."

I bury my face in her neck as I tug down her panties and let them drop to the floor. She smells so good my chest aches with it. When she widens her stance to step out of her panties, I slide my hand between her thighs and cup her bare sex. I know I've pushed her this far, but hell if I can find any remorse. "Fuck, Liz. I'm not going to be the good guy who walks away just because it's the right thing to do. Not tonight. If this isn't what you want, you have to tell me to stop."

She rocks into my touch. "What if this is exactly what I want?"

Her hands fumble between our bodies until the button on my pants releases and they fall to the floor. She shoves my briefs down next, then wraps her hand around my aching cock.

I can't wait. I'm blind with the need to be inside her.

Sliding my hands under her ass, I lift her up against the wall and slam into her in one long, hard motion.

She cries out, her nails digging into my back. "Yes," she whimpers. "Yes, please."

I soften my movements and slow my strokes. "Tell me what you want, Rowdy." My chest is tight, like a too-full balloon under the pressure of a life full of mistakes. One more fuck-up, one more shitty decision, and I'm going to explode.

She opens her eyes and brings one hand to my face as I pump into her. "You," she says. "I want you."

There's a knock at the door, and I still.

She squeezes tight around me. "Don't stop." My hips jerk, my orgasm coming too fast and too soon, and providing me with none of the relief I was looking for.

"Sam," a female voice calls from the other side of the door. "Open the door. I forgot my key."

* * *

Liz

He carefully withdraws and settles me to the ground. He drags a hand through his hair and turns his back to me as he takes jagged breaths.

What did we just do?

I push down my dress and grab my underwear from the floor. I don't know what that was, but it wasn't satisfying. Just desperate and needy, and not in the good way.

Jesus.

He steps into his pants and zips them up.

The knocking stops and his phone rings.

Sam grimaces then nods toward the bathroom. "Could you go in there for a minute?"

I gape at him, but someone's calling his name again so I go into the bathroom and shut the door behind me.

Breathless and frazzled, I listen as Sam opens the door.

"Hey," he says.

"You're shirtless," the female voice says. Is it Sabrina? "I like you shirtless."

"You two, please wait until I'm gone," a second female voice says. It might be Sam's mom, but I'm not sure. "I just wanted to say good night. I'm going to my room. Good to talk to you, Sabrina. Seeing you two together is just . . . I haven't been this happy in years."

Sam says good night, and the door opens and closes again.

"I thought you were already on the plane," Sam says.

"We're leaving in an hour," Sabrina says. "I'm heading up to Erin's room now, and I wanted make sure you don't want to come with us."

"I told you, I need to work."

She sighs heavily. "Okay. Take these back to your place for me?"

"Sure."

"We'll talk when I get back."

I wish I could see him. I want to see how he looks at her when no one else is watching. I want to know if he's touching her.

"What's that?" Sabrina asks.

"What?"

"You smell . . . you smell like perfume. *Women's* perfume."

"I'm sure I do. We danced all night."

The silence stretches for a long time, and again, I curse being stuck in this bathroom.

"I don't trust many people, Sam," Sabrina finally says. "And I've chosen to trust you. Please don't break my heart."

Then there's nothing but the *click* and *thunk* of the hotel room door closing.

I back away from the door, and seconds later, Sam's opening it, his eyes on the ground.

"Sorry." The word is so quiet I almost don't hear it. He's still not looking at me.

"About which part? The sex, or your *girlfriend*

interrupting us?"

"I should never have touched you tonight. It was a mistake."

My stomach claws its way up into my chest. "A mistake?" But of course it was. My gaze bounces around the room like a bird trying to find an open window, and it lands on a stack of women's clothes, neatly folded on a chair. A cry slips from my lips as I walk toward it. She changed here. "You're really with her." Of course he is. He never said otherwise, did he? I wanted to believe it was a sham, so I let him touch me. Let him fuck me.

He grabs my hand as I'm reaching for her shirt. "Liz, please."

I'm such a fool. Such a complete, naive fool. "You never said . . ."

"Isn't that how you prefer your men? Already attached?"

A fist in the solar plexus. "Fuck. You."

He flinches, but who cares? I'm out of here.

"Liz, stop. Just . . . please don't go. I crossed the line."

Hand on the door handle, I bow my head and swallow hard. "You did."

When I turn, his face is tilted up and he's rubbing his eyes with his palms. He drops his hands.

I shake my head. "I'm sorry." I don't know exactly what I'm apologizing for—or to whom. I close my eyes. They're useless words. This is what we've come to. Sam and I—a concept that held so much promise five months ago—have nothing more for each other than aimless anger and impotent apologies.

"Me too," he whispers. I see it in his eyes—that trapped look. Not the panicked look of a caged animal, but the misery of someone resigned to his shitty fate.

"If you're with her, really *with* her, not just fucking her, I deserve to know." My mind is at war—the conversation I just heard doesn't make sense in the context of the story I've been telling myself.

"Please don't break my heart."

"This wasn't your fault. What happened here, that's on me." He takes my face in his hands, his thumbs running along the length of my jaw. "But I don't think you and I should be around each other. I lose my head when you're close."

"Please tell me you didn't just cheat on your girlfriend with me." Hot tears roll down my cheeks. I feel cheap. Like dirt. The lowest kind of scum.

He drops his hands, and the loss of his warm touch makes my whole body go cold. "You should go."

"Sam? Please."

"It was a mistake, Liz. I promise it won't happen again.

CHAPTER NINE

Sam

"I CAN'T DO THIS."

Sabrina is sitting on the couch in Erin's suite, her legs crossed, her arms wrapped around her waist. She's not stupid. She knew I had someone in the bathroom and that's why she said the line about breaking her heart—she knew someone would hear her little show. From the look on her face you would have thought I betrayed an actual relationship with her, and not a pretend one. As soon as I got out of there, I came to the campaign manager's suite.

"Can't do what?" Erin asks. "Can't keep it in your

pants? You've made that clear."

"I can't pretend I'm with her." I point to Sabrina, and she flinches. I soften my voice. "I'm sorry." I lost my head having Liz so close to me after months of missing her desperately, and I'd been too busy getting off to say what I should have said. And then Sabrina showed up with my mother, and I realized I wasn't just putting my and Sabrina's secret at risk by having Liz there—I was risking hurting my mother all over again too.

I can't be responsible for that again, so I spared my mother and hurt Liz instead. I only wish I felt like that was the right decision.

"If you didn't want to be with her, you never should have recorded it," Erin says.

"Seriously?" I say. "You're going to sit there and pretend you don't know?"

Erin crosses her arms and sets her jaw. "Don't say it." I can see in her calculating eyes that she already knows.

"Why? Because if I say it here, I might say it to a journalist? You think I want the world to know the truth about that video? That I want to be labeled Governor Guy's former boy toy? Because that's what I was—almost a decade ago—I was a very consenting boy toy, and happy to be, but that was it."

Erin winces. "No. You see, you weren't. Let's get that straight from the start."

"We're going to rewrite history now?"

"Damn straight we are," Erin says.

I shake my head. "You think I'm going to go give

interviews? That I'm going sell my story? Trust me. I have no desire to tell the world about my sex life with Christine—"

"You mean your sex life with *Sabrina*," Erin says, her voice rising for the first time since I've met her.

"Stop." Sabrina squeezes her eyes shut and exhales slowly. "Sam, I'm sorry this sucks for you. I really am. We're just trying to make the best of a horrible situation. And you're right, this isn't our only choice, but we don't have many. And as much as Erin wants to play bad cop here, the truth is that this is your choice. *You* control what happens next. Either we continue as planned, pretending to be together, or you ruin Mom, or you ruin me. That's it. Those are our choices."

"It doesn't have anything to do with you," I say. "Why would it ruin you?"

"You don't want to continue to pretend to be with me, and you say you won't destroy Mom's political chances by telling the truth, so that leaves ruining me." She lifts her palms. "The whole world thinks I made a sex tape. A very *taboo* sex tape. And since, yeah, I've had a crush on you most of my life, it's a pretty convincing story. You act like I'm benefiting from this. Like I'm conning you into a big cover-up because it's great fun." She lifts her eyes to mine. They're wet with tears. "Did you know I was talking to a guy? I liked him. I thought . . ." She shakes her head. "But forget about me. I'm doing this for you, too. Because as much as you've hurt me by pretending I don't exist year after year, I still care about you, and I don't want your life to be defined by your affair with an older woman. They'll hound you if they learn the truth, Sam. You think *this* is bad? Just wait."

I drag a hand over my face and take a deep breath. She's right. I've been treating her like she benefits from this, when really she's the innocent victim.

"If they knew the truth," she says, "they would eat you alive. Even if you're a fucking asshole sometimes, you deserve better than that. And if you want any chance at a normal life, you need this to pass with as little fuss as possible."

I sink down onto the couch next to her. Jesus. I've had months to try to patch things up with Liz, but I waited until I *couldn't* have her.

Erin clears her throat. "Thankfully, they're assuming the video is recent and that the redhead is Sabrina. If the American people think that video is of Governor Guy, they'll never elect her to be their commander in chief."

"Her sex life is irrelevant to her political life," I mutter, but I know that's not true. Not to the voters.

"I managed to get you two an interview with Ina Turnstall for Monday," she says. "If you think you can get the woman you were with tonight to stay quiet, I think the interview could put a lot of questions to bed, no pun intended."

I feel sick. "Liz won't say anything."

Sabrina cocks her head at me. "It was *Liz*? Seriously? Even after what happened with your father?"

I go cold. "How do you know about that?"

She frowns. "Connor told me."

"Fuck," I mutter. "Asshole." I hate the idea of anyone knowing, but leave it to fucking Connor to share my family's private matters.

Erin rubs her temples. I'm pretty sure I'm gonna give her a heart attack. "I'd rather focus on you and Sabrina right now. Tell me you'll do it. One interview."

I look at Sabrina. "One interview where we lie to the world."

She tugs her bottom lip between her teeth. "Please, Sam?"

Erin flips her hair. "One interview where you tell the world the *truth* about your relationship and about how you're madly in love."

"The truth?" A humorless laugh slips from my lips, and the sound is ugly and empty. "I guess mine isn't the only family who doesn't understand the definition of *truth*." Sabrina looks so beaten down that I already know I'll do it, but regardless of what Sabrina and Erin think, I need to tell Liz the truth.

Liz

Sam: *We need to talk.*

"I'M SORRY IF I screwed up your date last night," Grace says, as she drives me to my apartment. "Dude, I was hammered."

"You didn't screw up my date." I close out the texting application and put my phone back in my purse.

I can't think of anything I want to hear from him, and I have no intention of replying.

I rub my eyes. I didn't sleep much. After leaving Sam's room, I went back to Grace's and took a long, hot shower, as if I could wash away the mistake of letting him touch me, letting him fuck me. *Use me.* When my skin was red from the hot water and my fingertips raisins, I turned off the tap and leaned against the cold tile, where I cried until I was too exhausted to cry anymore. Then I climbed into bed and attempted to sleep.

"So are you and sexy George a thing now?" she asks.

"No. I don't think I'm ready for that yet." My head is pounding and I wish she'd stop talking.

For a minute, I think she's heard my mental plea, because she's quiet for the first time since she got out of bed. Then she asks, "Who's the guy?"

I turn to her. "What?"

"The one who screwed you up? Is he back home?"

"Yeah. Someone back home. That's . . . why I left."

"I'm hoping you're about to tell me it's not Sam Bradshaw. I'm hoping you aren't hopelessly in love with the better half of Sambrina."

"Sambrina?"

"That's what they're calling them. Isn't it *special*? So, this is the part where you tell me he's not the reason you didn't screw Sexy Boy George's brains out, but I'm afraid I know better."

I keep my face neutral, unsure what to say.

She cuts her eyes to me. "We're going to need to

come up with a plan. If Sabrina knows you're still into her man, you're as good as fired."

"We don't need a plan. I'm not going to have anything to do with him." The words cut into me, but I force myself to say what I decided last night had to be. "Never again."

CHAPTER
TEN

Sam

I'M IN THE GREEN ROOM before our interview when my phone rings and I see my sister's name on the display.

"Hello?"

"Big day, big interview," Ryann says.

I'm surprised to get a call from my little sister before my television interview with Sabrina. The only time I've seen Ryann since the video leaked was briefly at the bank on Friday morning. Every time she looked at me, she feigned a gagging sound. Or maybe she was legitimately gagging, I don't know. Either way, she's more than a little disgusted to have seen an unwelcome picture of her big brother's sex life, so I didn't expect to hear from her today.

"Thanks, I guess. What do you need?"

"Just calling to say good luck before my brother's national television debut. Why is that weird?"

"Ryann?"

"I'm wondering if you called Liz. Or saw her. Or . . . anything. I'm wondering about Liz. Worrying about her, I guess." She sighs into the receiver. "God, I can't believe I'm even saying this, but I know about you and Christine." *Gag.* "I knew when it was happening." *Gag, gag.* "So I'm pretty sure that's an old video and it's not Sabrina. Not that I've watched it because . . ." More gagging.

"Never repeat that."

"I won't! God, I swear I'm not out to tell anyone, but I was hoping *you* would tell . . . someone."

"Who? Why?"

"Did you tell Liz?"

"I didn't." I cut my eyes across the room to where Sabrina is chatting up one of the producers. There's no doubt in my mind that she's concocting some doozy of a story about our first date or some shit.

"Why not?" Ryann asks.

"Because this has nothing to do with her, Ryann."

"I liked her," she says softly.

"Yeah, well, apparently that runs in the family." No need to pretend with Ryann. Ian told her everything about Dad's account. How Liz was supposed to meet Riverrat at the family cabin that night, but I showed up instead. She knows the whole sordid mess. I'm not sure how my father thought we *wouldn't* eventually find out, given he was using a program on which all of his children have administrative rights. Maybe he wanted me to know, since he likes to take things from me. Maybe Liz was just another power play.

"She thought he was you," Ryann says under her breath. The way she speaks so quietly makes me wonder if our mom is around. "And she stopped talking to him the minute she learned he wasn't. You *read* the transcript. You know this."

"I'm not having this conversation right now."

Sabrina cocks her head at me from across the room, worry creasing her brow. I attempt a reassuring smile.

"Call her," Ryann says. "Tell her the truth." Then she hangs up.

"Is everything okay?" Sabrina calls when I remove the phone from my ear.

"Just fine. Ryann was calling to wish us luck."

"She's such a sweetie!"

She returns to her conversation with the producer, and for the fortieth time today I pull up Lizzy's number on my phone. She's not replying to my texts or returning my calls, and my gut twists at the sight of her face. The image I assigned to her contact information is a snapshot I took while we were in Chicago. She's curled up with a book on the couch with one of my button-up shirts on and nothing else. Her hair falls in loose curls around her shoulders and the makeup's been washed from her face. She's fucking stunning just like that. I'm the world's biggest dumb-ass for letting things end the way they did Saturday night.

"You are *so handsome*."

I look up to see Sabrina crossing the room. She straightens my tie then smooths the lapels of my suit jacket. She's been awfully touchy-feely since we arrived at the studios in New York, and I've had one hell of a time not stepping away when I see her hands reaching for me. Then again, it seems like there have been cameras on us since we got off the plane, and I know she's giving this charade her best effort.

"Thank you. You look really . . . nice, too." She does. If I hadn't once thought of her as my lover's daughter, I might even say she's hot. Long legs, pink-painted lips, and curves on modest display in her pink dress.

She steps forward and loops her arms behind my neck. "Thank you for doing this," she whispers. Then, even quieter, "But if we're going to make this work, you need to stop staring at a picture of another woman." She presses even closer, and, rising onto her toes, brings her mouth to my ear. "And when you touch me, you need to act more like you're touching your lover and less like you're touching your grandmother."

I press a chaste kiss to her forehead. "I think they've seen enough of *us* touching, don't you?" I ask between clenched teeth.

She steps back, but her smile holds a warning.

"They're ready for you now," one of the network's employees announces. "Go ahead and take your seats. Ina will be out in a minute."

Erin arranged for our interview to be done with Ina Turnstall, national morning news personality known for her tearjerker interviews, and she coached us on how to best capitalize on what that audience responds to. We ironed out the details of a couple of key stories and a plan for fielding unexpected questions. It wasn't unlike being prepared to testify in court.

We're ushered into a big room where a couch and a couple of chairs are set up around a coffee table under the blaze of a dozen spotlights. The seating arrangement is one of those psychological games journalists like to play. Where will we sit? A chair each? One on the couch and one on the chair? Together? Close or with distance between us?

Sabrina squeezes my hand and directs me to the couch, though I'm smart enough to know this is the right choice without her leading me around like a puppy on a leash.

We don't have to wait long before Ina arrives and takes a seat in a chair across from us.

"Thank you so much for joining us," Ina says.

Sabrina beams. "Thank you for having us."

"I'm so excited we get to hear your big news with our audience first."

I look to Sabrina. What big news?

Liz

Someone pounds on my apartment door, and my

first thought is *Sam*.

But no. Even if I thought he'd come looking for me after what happened Saturday night, he wouldn't be here now. He has a televised interview at the WCBF network studio in approximately thirty minutes.

The pounding comes again, and I groan. In addition to the guy next door, I also live across the hall from a very nice, caring, thoughtful, and *nosy* old woman. If I'm not out of bed by eight on a Saturday morning, she's knocking on the door to make sure I'm still okay. If I run late for work one day, she knows it. She'll ask me as I get home that night, "Did you get reprimanded for being tardy?" And then of course there are her concerns about my love life. Or lack thereof . . .

My guess is that Mrs. Louise is bringing me dinner. She thinks I'm too skinny. And it's true, I guess. I've dropped some weight since I moved here. It's not that I don't know how to cook for myself—I can pop a frozen pizza in the oven as competently as the next girl—but I'm not hungry. Food does nothing but turn to ash in my mouth. I subsist mainly on coffee and the doughnuts that seem ever present at campaign headquarters.

With much reluctance, I go to the door. Last time Mrs. Louise brought me dinner, she sat at my kitchen table and watched to make sure I ate it. It was a broccoli casserole made with quinoa and black beans and spinach and carrots, and lots of healthy things that on their own might be good but together were kind of more than I could stand in a single day. The idea of another supervised dinner makes my stomach lurch in protest. Honestly, there are two kinds of eaters in this world: the kind who prefer Cheetos and daiquiris, and the kind Mrs. Louise cooks for. Since my idea of making healthier choices is choosing the strawberry Pop-Tart over the chocolate, it's safe to say I fall in the former category.

With a sigh, I walk to the door. I'll just tell her I already ate. I feel bad lying to her, but I would feel worse pretending I wasn't here. She's as lonely as I am.

I open the door without checking the peephole, but instead of Mrs. Louise, I see my best friends and sisters standing on the other side. Cally, Nix, Maggie, Krystal, and Hanna are all waiting with smiles on their faces.

"Surprise!" they chorus.

"You guys! What are you doing here?" My eyes burn with sudden tears. I've missed seeing them every day. I took that for granted when I lived in New Hope.

"Well," Hanna says, "if you won't visit us, we'll visit you."

"We missed you," Maggie says. "And we need to know what happened when you wore the fuck-me dress."

Nix lifts bags over her head and grins at me. "We have food, and we have booze."

The girls file into my teeny apartment and make their way to the little kitchen. They've been here before. They helped me move in when I found the place on the first of the year, and they've come by a couple of other times too. But they're right when they say I don't come home often. It's been more than five months since I moved to Indianapolis, and other than my panicked trip for wardrobe assistance on Saturday, I visit only when another lecture from my mom sounds more painful than the possibility of running into Sam.

After last night, I want to visit even less. Being close to Sam hurts too much, and looking my friends and sisters in the eye and seeing their pity? That hurts too.

"We brought comfort food," Krystal says. She opens the bags and pulls out oily boxes of onion rings, French fries, and mozzarella sticks. They must have picked them up on the way here, because the food is still steaming.

My stomach growls. Maybe I am a little bit hungry.

"We have beer," Cally says, "and we have wine."

"We left the hard stuff at home so we won't be tempted to get drunk," Nix says. "It still might be tempting. But one of us has to drive home."

"You could stay," I offer hopefully.

The three married ladies all look at their hands awkwardly, and I know without them saying that they want to get home to their men. Cally and Hanna probably want to get home to their babies as well.

"I have rounds at the hospital in the morning," Nix says. "Or I totally would."

"I need to open up the bakery," Krystal says. "And Hanna is working on the *prettiest* cake for a wedding this weekend."

I wave a hand. "It's no big deal." But it kind of is. It hurts to see their lives moving forward without me, even if, intellectually, I know that's unfair.

Maggie digs through my cabinets, producing plates for our fried buffet and glasses for our drinks.

I pile my plate with more food than I know I can eat.

As inconspicuously as possible, I keep my eye on the TV running quietly in the living room. I don't plan on missing Sam's interview.

I sigh as I survey the junk food and alcohol. The only thing missing is a heartbroken fool spilling her guts. Might as well get that going too. "I went to Sam's hotel room Saturday night."

Hanna drops her plate on the counter, and Nix coughs into her beer.

"Well, that was unexpected," Krystal says.

"What happened?" Hanna asks.

"We had sex." To my horror, my eyes fill with tears. "Sabrina showed up, and he made me hide in the bathroom. I think they might be serious. Not just . . ." I draw in a shaky breath. "Not just fucking."

"But he fucked *you*," Maggie says.

I nod. "She accused him of smelling like another woman's perfume and then said, 'Don't break my heart.'" I shake my head. "I feel so dirty."

Krystal props her hands on her hips. "Bastard."

"Neither of us meant for it to go that far. It was a mistake."

"A mistake?" Nix breaks a mozzarella stick in two. "So, his dick just fell into you? Like, *oops*?"

Cally twists the top off a beer and presses the cold drink into my hand. "Drink this."

She watches me carefully until I take two long slugs from the bottle. It's a light beer—crisp, refreshing—and my stomach wants to push it right back up.

When the bottle is half drained, Cally takes my shoulders in her hands. "I am *not* convinced there's anything serious between Sam and Sabrina." She must see my grimace, because she says, "I'm serious. Will said Sam was *very* weird about the whole Sabrina thing. He thinks their relationship is a lie, and so does Max. They're his best friends, and I trust their instincts on this."

I want to believe that. God, I do. Even if there's no future for Sam and me, I don't want to be the other woman again. And I don't want Sam to be the kind of man who would do that to his girlfriend.

"What did he say after Sabrina left?" Hanna asks.

"He apologized and said it was a mistake."

"Did you ask what the deal is with him and Sabrina?" Krystal asks.

I nod. "He didn't answer, really, but when she was talking to him it was clear that they're together."

"I want to talk to him," Hanna says.

"Han—"

She holds up her hand to stop me. "He's hurt my sister enough. Now I want some answers. You deserve answers."

I put down my untouched plate and stare at the television, where they're playing an intro to the Sam and Sabrina interview. The girls follow my gaze.

"Wanna hear it?" Nix asks.

I nod, and she grabs the remote and turns up the volume.

If I thought I was okay with this in any way, if I thought I'd made my peace with Sam being with someone else, the first words out of the interviewer's mouth prove me wrong.

SOMETHING REAL

"Congratulations on your engagement!"

CHAPTER
ELEVEN

Liz

"I TAKE IT BACK," Hanna says. "I take back every nice thing I ever said about him. And even some of the not-so-nice-but-not-quite-mean-enough things too. Piece-of-shit scumbag."

I would gape at my twin, who usually doesn't talk like that, but I'm too busy gaping at the television.

"We should turn it off," Krystal says. "Nothing good will come of watching this."

Cally reaches for the remote, but I stop her with a hand on her forearm. "No, I want to see it."

I tear my gaze away from the TV to see the girls all

exchange a look, as if I'm going to let them decide whether or not I torture myself with this interview. They should know me well enough to know that if they try to turn off that TV, I'm going to kick them the fuck out of my apartment.

Engaged. He's engaged.

He didn't cheat on his girlfriend with me. He cheated on his *fiancée.*

"I'm watching it," I say firmly, and they sigh but don't fight me.

I sink into the couch and stare at the screen. Sam is looking at the interviewer, a grimace on his face. I wonder what he's thinking. Does he hate this? How public his life has become? Or is he just thinking about how quickly he can get Sabrina alone again, get her naked and tie her up? Maybe he's worried I'm going to tell her what happened and ruin this for him.

"Well, we aren't exactly—" Sam begins.

Sabrina jumps in. "Who told our secret?" She turns to Sam. "I thought we weren't going to tell yet?"

He reaches up and tucks a lock of her hair behind her ear. I think I'd rather have him kick me in the face.

Sabrina looks back to Ina. "It's hard, you know, falling in love with so many eyes on you. I didn't want to make a spectacle of our relationship, and Sam here kept telling me he was done being so secretive." She squeezes Sam's hand. "What was it you said last month? You wanted to 'shout it from the rooftops'?" She tugs her lip between her teeth and breathes a dreamy sigh.

She's so damn pretty. I don't normally find myself

comparing my looks to those of other women. Insecurities are Hanna's department. It's not that I think I'm all that, but I grew up watching Hanna feel bad about her looks. I know damn well that she's beautiful, so her insecurities taught me that beauty comes in all packages and I should appreciate mine for what it is.

Whether or not I was the prettiest girl in the room never mattered much to me. I always believed there would be a guy who thought I was prettier than anyone else in the whole world, just because I'm me. I didn't need every guy I met to think I was beautiful. I just wanted to, someday, with some guy, be the prettiest girl in the room to *him*.

Sam did that for me. I wonder if he makes Sabrina feel the same way.

"I think it's just precious that you two were trying to keep your relationship quiet." You can tell the host is so damn psyched to have this interview that it's all she can do to keep from bouncing in her seat.

Sam, on the other hand, looks as if he'd rather be hung by his toenails. "It was what Sabrina wanted," Sam says. "And I respected that. Until someone took that decision from our hands, that is."

"Well, you two made it clear that you won't talk about the tape during this interview, but can you tell me what you thought when it was first leaked? And are you worried about who leaked it?"

Sabrina laughs. "My first thought was, 'My mom's going to see this.'" The women laugh together then Sabrina's face goes serious. "We don't know who's responsible for the leak, but my laptop was hacked a couple weeks ago. We thought someone was looking for campaign secrets, but look what they found instead."

"It was a violation of our privacy," Sam says. "We're still reeling."

Ina nods sagely. "Shall we talk about how you met? Sabrina gave us these pictures." The screen cuts to images of Sam and Sabrina when they were young: a bare-chested, younger Sam sitting on the edge of the pool, and awkward, gap-toothed Sabrina sitting next to him. The way she's looking at him, you can tell she's crushing hard. But Sam seems completely oblivious to her.

In the next picture, the two look as if they're on their way to prom or something. Sabrina's in a big froofy dress that swallows her up, and Sam's in a suit and tie. Other images follow—the two at family gatherings, political balls, fundraisers, and cookouts, and in almost every image, Sabrina seems to be gazing longingly at Sam, and Sam seems to be clueless to her existence.

When they cut back to the couple in the studio, Sabrina is giving Sam one of those puppy-dog-love looks again. Only this time, she has his hand in hers and he's looking right back at her. I want to believe that what he has on his face isn't love, that it isn't adoration. I want to believe he's looking at the product of political convenience. Once the sex-tape scandal has settled, his relationship with Sabrina might even be good for the campaigns—Christine's and Mr. Bradshaw's.

Only I'm not convinced this is a political move. Sam wasn't interested in using his personal life to advance his father's career. But still, my gut tells me I'm missing something, that Sam would never have had sex with me on Saturday when he planned to marry another woman.

My brain says I'm delusional and have horrible taste in men.

Frankly, I still haven't wrapped my head around the fact that he never called. I moved up here and started my new job, but in all other ways my life was on hold, as I waited for Sam to forgive me. I know I could've called him, but it didn't feel as if I had the right. So I wrote that letter instead.

I carried that letter in my purse for weeks, feeling like the biggest coward in the world because I couldn't bring myself to put it in the mailbox. But now he's getting married, and I'm grateful I never sent it. I have waking nightmares of Sabrina reading the letter and laughing with Sam about how stupid I am.

"I think I've always loved Sam," Sabrina says. "Our families have been close for years, so we grew up around each other. He'd come to our house in the summers, and here I was, this dorky, awkward teenage girl. He was this hunky, slightly older football player. I was lost."

"Gag me," Krystal says. "Are they for real?"

Hanna wrinkles her nose. "I can't put my finger on it, but there's something I don't like about her."

"I don't believe it," Cally says, shaking her head. "He's in love with Liz. This just doesn't add up."

It's a small comfort that Cally is suffering from the same delusions I am.

"And what did you think about *her,* Sam?" Ina asks.

Sam grins at Sabrina and rubs his thumb across her bare shoulder. "I think we spend our lives looking for something special. Us lucky ones find it was right in front of our eyes the whole time. It sounds clichéd, but I can tell you it's the truth."

The TV goes black, and I look around the room until I find Nix holding the remote. "No more," she says. "You look like someone's killing your puppy right in front of you, and I won't watch you torture yourself like that. As your doctor, I forbid it."

I don't argue. I'm too spent. A couple of minutes of interview were more than I could stand. "You guys, thanks for coming, but I think I just need to be alone right now."

"No," Krystal says. "Absolutely not. I've been here before. What you need is to go out and have fun with your friends. Drinks and dancing, and then maybe a make-out session with a random guy—but don't go home with him. That will just make you feel bad about yourself in the morning."

Maggie arches a brow. "You don't say."

Krystal shrugs. "Like I say, I speak from experience. We're here and we can help. Let us. Where's your favorite place to drink?"

"Brady's," Hanna answers for me. "And since we know there's no danger of running into Sam, I think that's exactly where we should go."

* * *

Sam

"What the fuck was that?"

Across from us in the limo, Erin crosses her long legs and smirks. "*That* was entertainment. *That* was getting America's attention off that video and onto something that won't screw up our lives, something everyone loves—a wedding. With minimal help from our social media team, the Sambrina hashtag was trending on Twitter before the interview was even over."

"*Sambrina?* Jesus. I didn't agree to be her fiancé."

"You aren't," Sabrina says. She crosses her legs and arms and looks out the window. Her body language is the opposite of what it was in the studio. Closed instead of open. Cold instead of warm. "Do you think I'd want to marry you after seeing that video? I'd like to think I can do better than my mom's sloppy seconds, thank you very much."

"Enough," Erin says. "The interview was great, and we're turning a political nightmare into a win. We'll see what the pollsters come back with tomorrow, but I would bet we'll be trending upward in no time. Let's focus on that."

"I'm sorry," Sabrina says, dropping her gaze to her lap. "You're right, Erin, and I'm sorry."

Maybe she's right about the campaign, but this isn't

just about the campaign anymore. Now it's about my life. Now it's about Liz believing I'm engaged to another woman. The idea of her watching the interview cuts into me, and there's nothing I want more than to fix the whole mess.

"You're going to have to do this without me," I say, holding up my hands. "I agreed to one interview and you fucked me over."

Erin cocks her head and studies me for a beat, then she draws a manila folder from her briefcase and tosses it on my lap. "Is that really what you think?"

I open the envelope and my stomach drops. A picture of Asia's little girl is paper-clipped to the top of a stack of papers. "What? How?"

"We do our research," Erin says. "Go ahead and look through it. You'll find a DNA test confirming that you're her father."

I flip through the pages. "How did you . . ."

"Connor told us," Sabrina says.

"What *hasn't* he told you?"

She shrugs. "He was worried it might come up when the sex tape broke. He used to be an intern for my mother, and he still gives us information when he thinks it's relevant."

"Don't underestimate my connections, Sam," Erin says. "I'm good at what I do because I'm thorough. I get things done."

I swallow. I don't know how they got my DNA for the test, or the child's. I'm not sure I want to know.

"Erin likes to sound big and bad," Sabrina says. "But what she's *trying* to say is that this is for you too. You want to meet your daughter, don't you? Maybe have some visitation rights someday?"

I shake my head. "No court would—"

"No, the court wouldn't," Erin says. "Especially after that unsavory tape. But we have connections to the girl's family. If you make nice and plan a wedding to Sabrina, we'll use those connections so you can meet your daughter."

I can't take my eyes off the picture and those big brown eyes staring back at me.

"Her name's Lilly," Sabrina says softly. "She looks like a *Lilly,* doesn't she?"

"Help us paint the picture of a man in love, Sam," Erin says. "Make it easy for the family to let Lilly meet her daddy."

I lift my eyes to meet Sabrina's. She gives a soft smile. "We'll be America's sweethearts. I'm not saying it will be easy, but if you do this for us, we'll do that for you. It's the least we can do."

"So what do we do now?" I ask, and my voice squeaks a little. "How long do we carry on pretending to be engaged?"

"At least through the election," Erin says. "But you two are cute together. Why not give it a shot?"

Sabrina sighs. "If she doesn't win, we can quietly split after and no one will care. If she wins, we should probably wait until after the inauguration to break up. If we start planning a wedding for a year and a half from now, no one would think that's strange. It's normal for more elaborate weddings to get a longer lead time, but actual wedding plans will give the media something pretty to focus on."

Sure, the media will love it, but what does Liz think? Fuck, she probably doesn't care. After Saturday, I'm sure the only thing she wants to do is cut off my balls.

I rub the back of my neck. "Don't you have better things to do than plan a pretend wedding?" I ask Sabrina.

She smiles. "Sure. Aside from Erin, I'm the best political mind on my mother's entire campaign. I'd rather be putting my skills to work for her than pretending to be engaged to you, but potato, po-*tah*-to."

She's good at the political BS. She always had a mind for it. "Any plans for a future in politics?"

She snorts. "Any plans I had were blown to pieces the second I agreed to pretend that video was of me and not my mom."

I drop my gaze back to the big brown eyes of the child in the picture. How can such a little thing mean so much to me when I've never met her?

CHAPTER TWELVE

Liz

"I'M SO DRUNK," I singsong, my arms around Hanna's neck, "a vampire would get a buzz on a shot of my blood."

She quirks a brow. "A vampire?"

"That should totally be a roadside sobriety test. Police officers could drive around with vampires in the back seat. Like Alexander Skarsgård."

"I think you mean Eric Northman," Hanna says, leading me back to our booth.

"Isn't that what I said?"

"Skarsgård is the actor; Northman's the vampire."

"See what I'm saying? I'm so drunk, I'm struggling

to comprehend the difference."

Hanna grins. She has such a pretty smile. Definitely the prettiest of my sisters.

"Thanks a lot," Krystal mutters, but Maggie just laughs and says, "It's probably true. I'm cool with that assessment."

"I said that out loud?"

Nix slides a full glass of water in front of me. "You haven't even had that much to drink. Have you eaten anything today?"

"Eat this," Hanna says. She plops a plate in front of me that has two croissants, chocolate peeking out from their centers, and a scone of some sort on it.

"Brady's is serving your baked goods now?" I ask.

"Not officially, but he's keeping some stuff stocked on a trial basis. The scone is savory, not sweet. Garlic, sharp cheddar, and rosemary."

I start with that one and moan around my first bite. "You're a goddess."

"Those are pretty popular here," Hanna says, "but they hardly move at the bakery. I think people come to the bakery with a sweet tooth, but they want salty stuff while they're drinking. If I can convince Brady to stock my stuff regularly, I'd have a chance to make a bigger variety."

"He'll do it," Krystal says. "No question. He's trying to hardball me on the contract, but he has no idea who he's working with."

By the time the scone's gone, and I take a bite of the croissant, I'm starting to feel less drunk. Good in theory, I suppose, but with less drunk comes less happy.

Boo.

"Thanks for bringing me here tonight, ladies." My eyes might be watering a little. Allergies, I'm sure. "You were right. I needed a girls' night." And I needed to come home. Indianapolis is great, but New Hope is home, and a sick heart needs to be home.

"I'm going to head out, actually," Cally says apologetically. "I have an early client. You wanna come with me, Liz? You can totally crash in our guest bedroom."

"Or mine," Hanna says. "I need to get going too. If the twins wake up in the middle of the night, they insist on having Mommy."

"I should at least get a nap before opening the bakery." Krystal sighs. "I'd offer for you to stay at my place, but I don't have a guest room. I'm so ready to upgrade to a house. The market is just crap right now."

"You're welcome at our place, too," says Maggie.

"And mine," Nix says. "And I can stick around here a little longer if you want."

I point to each of my friends and sisters. "Eeny-meeny-miny-moe." Then I grin and point to Nix. "I'll stay with her. Single chicks unite."

"Damn straight," she mutters.

The girls gather their things and head out, leaving Nix and me alone in the previously cramped booth.

"Don't you have rounds in the morning or something?" I ask.

"Oh, girl, I've been to med school. My body is trained to run on very little sleep." She leans forward onto her elbows. "I'm glad you're coming home with me. I rattle around in that place. Maybe the mortgage will feel like less of an abomination if I know someone else has used one of the rooms."

"Thanks for having me. When I'm in Indy, sometimes I forget what good friends I have back home." Yep. Sobriety is a downer, all right. I put the rest of the croissant back on the plate and push it aside. Suddenly, every movement takes far more effort than it should and nothing sounds better than closing my eyes. "Actually, would you be okay with heading out soon? It just hit me how tired I am."

"Sure, let me use the restroom and we can go." She slides out of the booth, and I study the bar. There's a pretty good crowd, considering it's after midnight on a weeknight and the college kids have gone home for the summer. The people filling the tables and lingering around the bar are people I've known my whole life.

What am I going to do when the campaign is over? Find another job in Indy? Try to find something in DC?

What I really want is to come back to New Hope, but I can't do that if Sam is here. Maybe he and Sabrina will live somewhere else. Would he leave his job at the bank? And if they live here, will I ever get over it? Will there be a time when I could watch them walk down the street, children in tow, and not feel as if I'm being torn apart?

"Sam!" someone calls, and I think I'm imagining it at first—my liquor-addled brain imagining the word it's thinking of. But then I hear it again, and I see him talking to Brady at the bar.

As if he can sense me, he turns. The second his eyes

land on me, he flinches.

Right back at ya, buddy.

My stomach cramps. It *hurts* to have him this close. And yet I want him to come talk to me almost as desperately as I want to disappear.

He says something else to Brady, then he walks toward my table. Is he really coming over here? Crap. He is.

He's standing right here, looking down at me as if I'm supposed to say something, as if he expects me to remember how to speak when he's standing so close I can smell him.

"You're avoiding my calls," he says.

"With good reason."

"May I sit?"

"You sure your fiancée would approve of you sitting with your . . ." I almost say *ex-girlfriend,* but that sounds too pathetic. "With another woman?"

He slides into the opposite side of the booth. "Yeah, I'm sure."

I look away. *Shit.* I was so proud of myself for that standoffish, *fuck you very much* response, and look where it got me—sitting across from the only person who can make me feel worse than I already do.

"I didn't expect to see you here," he says, his words gentle when I expected accusatory.

"I could say the same for you," I say. "Aren't you supposed to be in New York?"

"We flew home right after the interview. Sabrina has an important meeting in the morning."

"Good for her."

He shakes his head. "Never mind about Sabrina. I'm glad you're here. I think we should talk."

I close my eyes at the sound of his voice. I'm still drunk; it's true. But even sober, I'm pretty sure I'd be tempted to bottle that voice and take it home with me. *Sweet torture.*

"I need to ask you a favor."

His rich honey eyes lock with mine. For a minute I picture myself giving him anything he wants. I picture myself being his secret mistress after he marries Sabrina. I picture myself living a despicable life that leaves me empty in every moment I'm not with him. Maybe it would be worth it—if only to be alive for those moments when we were together instead of dead every second of every day.

"What you *need* to do is walk away and never talk to me again." The words don't come out hard like they should. Instead, they're soft and tentative, each one a drip from a tap that fills my throat with tears.

I will *not* cry.

"Hey," Nix says behind me. "I can't leave you alone for—*oh.* Sam. You're supposed to be in New York."

"I came back. I need a minute alone with Liz." He never takes his eyes off me. "Please hear me out?"

"Er, um." Nix checks over each shoulder as if she's looking for backup. I'm sure that, like me, she's wishing the other girls hadn't left yet.

"It's okay," I tell her. But it's really not. I'm about to have that conversation where he tells me he's moved on and that he's really happy with Sabrina. That Saturday night was a mistake and he'd appreciate it if I didn't tell anyone. Maybe he'll say he was drunk, or maybe he'll say there was no excuse for whispering dirty words in my ear and making me think he's missed me as much as I've missed him.

"There's so much you and me, there's no air left when we share a room. There's always you and me."

Nix clears her throat. "I'll be at the bar if you need me."

Sam watches her go. "She hates me."

"She's my friend. Hating you is part of the job description."

When he returns his eyes to mine, there's vulnerability in them that I don't want to see. "And what about you?" he asks.

"I'm pretty sure the way we feel about each other became irrelevant the second you asked Sabrina to marry you." Yep. Definitely too drunk to have this conversation.

"I'd rather not talk about this here. Can we go outside? I can explain everything. Please?"

"That depends. Did you fuck me while you were engaged to another woman?"

He stares at me for a long time, and for the life of me I feel as if he's trying to tell me something telepathically—my untrustworthy gut at work again.

Ultimately, his silence is more painful than any answer I can imagine.

I swallow. "Congratulations, by the way. You are officially your father's son."

SOMETHING REAL

✳ ✳ ✳

Sam

The words drive into me like the dull blade they were meant to be. "Touché."

"So, you and Sabrina. That's . . . You told me your dad wanted to set you up, and look at you now. On your way to the altar." She gives a wobbly smile. "How nice for your family."

Does she really believe I'm going to marry Sabrina when I was confessing my love for her five months ago? Does she think love comes that easily for me? "We need to talk."

"Isn't that what we're doing now?"

She looks beautiful tonight. She's in a tank top with those skinny straps, her hair's down, draping over her bare shoulders, and her cheeks are flushed. In a simpler world, we'd be on the same side of the booth, laughing instead of mincing our words. I'd be touching her under the table, teasing her with my fingers against her leg and my words in her ear until she was wet and begging me to finger her right here in the middle of the bar.

Something knots in my chest. I try to swallow it down and can't. "I mean really talk. In private."

"I thought you didn't think we should be around each other. What was it you said? I make you lose your head? Because, you know, I'm the woman, so what happened between us is completely my fault. You're just a poor, vulnerable man who should be expected to think with his penis."

I'm almost glad to see her so angry with me. It beats the broken woman I turned my back to on Christmas Day. "There are things I need to say, to tell you."

"Go for it. Say what you need to say so we can get away from each other."

"Have you told anyone about Saturday night?"

She swallows. "A couple of people."

"Fuck, Liz." I hate this. I hate lying to her and I hate asking her to keep our night together quiet, like she's my dirty little secret. I want her to know the truth about Sabrina and the engagement, but it would be too much of a gamble to tell her here. Too many big ears and curious eyes. We've probably already said too much. I lower my voice to a hushed whisper. "No one can know. I know it's not fair to you, but—"

"Don't worry," she says. "No one will tell. It's not exactly something I'm proud of. Now if there's nothing else, I need to leave. I don't like who I am when you're around."

Using every bit of self-control I have, I keep my hands to myself as she climbs out of the booth.

It's a good thing she moved away after Christmas, or I never would have stayed away from her. Two minutes near her, and I want to . . . what?

Yell at her for not telling me about her online affair with Riverrat.

Take her to the bathroom and fuck her against the wall, making sure to get her off so she'll remember how good it was between us.

Explain how her relationship with my father broke me in a way no one else can fix.

Drive her back to my place and slowly undress her. Kiss her slowly and all over until she's trembling, and promise things I can't deliver.

Take her hands in mine and tell her that I'm sorry for acting like an ass and that she deserves better.

Beg her to move home.

Ask her to stay away.

I am the scum of the earth. The hurt is all over her face, whether she's trying to hide it or not. Maybe a few months ago I believed she deserved that, but tonight I just want to take back everything I've ever done to hurt her.

I need a drink.

"Goodbye, Sam." She slides out of the booth and stands, giving me a view of her long, lean legs exposed in her short skirt. Why isn't there anything in this universe I want as much as I want her?

"Liz," I call as she starts to leave. She stops, and for a second I think I'd say anything to keep her from walking away. *I'm not really engaged . . . There's nothing between Sabrina and me . . .*

I'm sorry.

But she's not interested in listening and this isn't the place, so all I say is, "I'm sorry. For everything."

She stops but doesn't look at me. "Thank you."

What I would give to see her look at me the way she did on Christmas—eyes full of love, and the words on her lips. "You always deserved better than me anyway."

CHAPTER THIRTEEN

Liz

"Don't you think it's a little weird that he came back to town tonight?"

I frown. I've slept like crap since the night at the Conrad, and I might just be too tired to understand what Nix is saying. She's my new favorite person, because not only is she making me coffee, she has a loaf of Hanna's cinnamon raisin bread that she toasted up with apple butter for a midnight snack. I couldn't be friends with those women who have declared carbs their mortal enemies.

"How was it weird?" I ask.

"Not just him coming back," she says. "Their whole relationship, really. No one in this town can take a shit without the *Tattler* reporting it to the world, and yet somehow Sam and Sabrina have been carrying on in a very intense relationship the last five months—one so deeply emotional they'd have us believe they want to get married—and no one noticed?"

I get that niggling feeling again. The one that comes from my untrustworthy gut. "But what does that have to do with him being at Brady's tonight?"

She shrugs. "I don't know. It's more of the same. They did the interview, but then they went their separate ways. They're engaged? Seriously? I'm not jumping to Sam's defense. As far as I'm concerned, he can suck goat testicles for the way he treated you Saturday, but I don't know. Their engagement sounds more like a ploy to make their kinky pics more palatable. Even then, they don't even act like *lovers*, ya know? Like, why come to Brady's tonight when you can stay in Indianapolis and fuck Sabrina Guy?" She snorts. "God, what if that video isn't even *of* Sam and Sabrina? What if the ginger is Governor Guy or something? Somehow *that* seems more believable to me."

"Governor Guy wouldn't be that careless during . . ." I put my hand over my mouth. Guy wouldn't be that careless during a campaign, but what about *before* her campaign? What about a decade ago, before she cut her hair, before she was even governor and before the stress of politics started to show on her face?

"I know!" Nix says, laughing and totally missing my

shock. "I'm totally joking. But it's hilarious to think about, isn't it?"

"Pretty sure I'd lose my job if I was caught laughing at any such joke." I'm trying to sound light, but now that my mind has latched on to this crazy idea, I can't think of anything else. It's ridiculous. Wishful thinking.

But didn't Sam tell me he'd lost his virginity with an older woman? A family friend whom he'd watch when he spent summers at her pool?

"Nix, may I use your computer?"

"Sure, go for it. It's on the desk in the office. I have to head to bed. Early morning rounds await. Make yourself at home and wake me if you need anything."

I nod, mentally willing her to bed so I can use her computer without her looking over my shoulder.

I nibble my toast until she finally leaves. As soon as she closes her bedroom door, I'm practically running to the computer to pull up the pictures of him and "Sabrina."

It's really hard to tell much from the images that have been published on the news sites. There's no good shot of her face. I need to see the whole video, but none of the networks have it readily available.

After a little web searching and some poking around on the kind of sites that may or may not infect Nix's computer with crippling viruses, I'm able to find the footage from the sex tape itself, rather than just the stills.

As much as I don't want to watch Sam have sex with another woman, I can't let this go, so I push play on the video and I watch. Ten minutes later, I'm convinced the footage isn't new.

Sam is muscular in the video, but I've spent enough time with him naked to know he's smaller in this video than he is now. And though there's not a clear enough shot of the woman to prove she *isn't* Sabrina, Sam doesn't move with the confidence of the experienced lover he is now. One thing is clear to me: the video is old.

I clear the browser's history and close the computer.

The world has its hands on a sex tape of Sam and a major presidential candidate from when Sam was close but not *quite* legal. His engagement has to be a cover-up. Is that why he wanted to talk to me tonight? Was he going to tell me the truth?

I want to believe—maybe too badly—that Sam wouldn't have had sex with me if his engagement to Sabrina were real. He's better than that.

As someone who works for the Guy campaign, the truth is irrelevant. All that matters is the script we create, and it'll be my job to do everything I can to perpetuate the "Sambrina love story," even if I believe it to be a lie.

As the woman who he had up against the wall in his hotel room last week, the truth is everything. I have to know.

You deserve to know the truth. And if you're wrong,

Sabrina deserves to know the truth. This isn't about getting Sam back.

I lift my hand to knock on Sam's door, then drop it again. My stomach twists and flips. I walked here from Nix's. Using a small flashlight and a lot of questionable judgment, I walked here in the middle of the night because I have to know.

So, here I am. At Sam's house to ask him to tell me what could possibly be the biggest secret he has.

"*Stupid, stupid, stupid,*" I mutter. Stupid to come, stupid to think this might go any way but badly, stupid to hope.

Finally, I make myself knock. Sam opens the door in nothing but a towel and a scowl.

He does a double take when he sees me. I don't know whom he expected to see at his door in the middle of the night, but the way his expression changes makes it clear I wasn't it.

For a minute we just stare at each other. I don't know what it's like for him, but I'm just standing here trying to remember how to breathe, trying not to wrap my arms around him and take in his smell.

"Liz," he says. "You came."

I swallow hard. I want to say, *You said you loved me.* I want to say, *Love should be enough.* But I'm not here to make some dopey attempt at a reunion that could never work. I'm here for the truth.

Sam turns around without waiting for my response and heads into the house, leaving the door open behind him. I'm not sure whether he's too disgusted at the sight of me to bother with closing the door, or if he expects me to follow him inside. I take a chance and follow, shutting the door behind me.

The living room is tidy, save for a basket of unfolded laundry sitting on the couch and a few empty beer bottles on the kitchen island.

Sam heads straight to his bedroom. "I have to get dressed." But two steps before he reaches the door, he stops and turns to me. "You were probably right. It's a bad idea for us to be alone together."

"Probably."

"What changed your mind?"

My mouth has gone dry, my breathing ragged. Will I ever meet another man whose proximity can make me feel so much? "I came for Sabrina. And for me."

He smiles then. But it's not the nice smile that I remember. This is the cruel, sardonic smile of a man who has no faith in the world. "For *Sabrina*? So you're her little errand girl? How'd that happen?"

"You fucked me. If your relationship with her is real, if you are really marrying her, she deserves to know the truth about what happened at the Conrad." I watch his face, but there's no sign there as to what he thinks of my threat.

"Come here."

"What?"

"Just—" He shakes his head and crosses back to me in three long strides. One hand comes into my hair and the other slides around my waist. His palm slips under my tank, hot on the small of my back. He lowers his face until it's two inches from mine. Our breath mingles. "I can't decide if I want to kiss you stupid or throw you out of my house," he murmurs against my mouth.

He smells like soap, his skin hot and still damp from the shower, his hair wet. The hard lines of his chest are still damp, and if he wrapped his arms around me now, I wouldn't be able to smell anything but him. I wait for the kiss that I'm sure is coming. Because I am weak.

"I don't want you thinking that I'm just like my father. I can't . . ." He closes his eyes and rubs the tip of his nose against mine in a gesture that is so innocuously intimate it breaks my heart.

He steps back without kissing me, eyes raking over me as if he's trying to figure me out. "You can tell Sabrina whatever you want. She already knows. She knew that night when she smelled your perfume."

Sam

I can't have her here. There's no part of Liz being in my house in the middle of the night that says "good idea." But in the battle between my brain and every other piece of me, my brain isn't even putting up a fight.

She licks her lips. "I want you to tell me the truth. About the video. About Christine Guy."

I wait for the panic to hit, but it doesn't. I've wanted to tell her the truth from the beginning, and sending her away on Saturday night without explaining was worse than any consequence that could come from her knowing.

Foolish or not, I trust Liz with this, and instead of panic, her suggestion that she knows the truth fills me with relief. I don't want to lie to her, and I couldn't live with the idea of her feeling like I'd made her the other woman. I couldn't live with her believing I'm no better than my father. "You watched the video."

"The whole world watched it," she says.

"And?"

"It's old. You're younger, not as muscular. Maybe she's your fiancée, maybe not, but either way, Sabrina is not the woman in that video."

"Is that what you think?"

She nods. "Yes. I think the video is of you and someone with whom such a video would prove *much more* scandalous."

Yeah. She knows. "Are you planning on sharing these suspicions with anyone?"

"Of course not!" Her eyes go wide and her lips part. "I told you, I'm here for Sabrina as much as I am for me."

"You keep using her as an excuse to come to me in the middle of the night."

She frowns. "It's not an excuse. I thought I slept with an engaged man. I deserve to know."

"Yeah? And how long did you lie in bed thinking about me before you let yourself come here? How long did you think about *this*?" I lower my mouth to hers and kiss her.

When my lips sweep over hers, it's as if life is my malady and Liz is the only cure. Tension unwinds from my shoulders and my gut releases its constant clench. For the moments my mouth is on hers, all is right with the world.

Until she presses both hands against my bare chest and shoves me away.

"Don't!"

I take a step back to catch my balance.

"Don't touch me. Regardless of what you think of me, I'm not the horrible woman who would sleep with another woman's fiancé. Stop putting me in this position." Her face crumbles, and I flinch. I've been such an ass.

"Liz." I gather her into my arms, and she starts to push me away again. "Rowdy, listen. There's nothing between me and Sabrina but a fabricated engagement to appease the millions of people who watched a very old, very private video."

When she looks up at me, tears have gathered in her lashes. "I'm right? The engagement's not real?"

I wipe a tear from each rosy cheek. Christ, this woman owns my soul. "We're just trying to make the best of a shitty situation. I'm sorry you got caught in the middle."

She rests her head on my chest and groans. "You made me feel like shit."

"I know." I smooth her hair down and kiss the top of her head. "I'm sorry. My mom showed up with Sabrina, and I panicked. My family doesn't even know the truth, but I wanted to tell you."

"Why are you doing it? I mean, I understand why you're telling everyone it's Sabrina, but why the fake engagement?"

"Sabrina was screwed over by her own mother's political pursuits. She had nothing to do with that video, but she has to let the world think it's her because her mom wants to be president. I understand what that's like."

She nods. "So either she gets to be the punch line of late-night comedians' dirty sex-tape jokes, or you play along to a further degree and she's just a woman who had kinky sex with her fiancé."

"The difference may not seem like much, but it's huge."

She wraps both of her arms around my waist. Damn, that feels good. "I get it," she whispers.

"My dad is a cheater, Liz. In retrospect, it's so obvious that this has been his pattern. I chose not to see the other women. That's just who he is. He's got a lot of qualities, but fidelity isn't one of them. And you know what? As much as I hate that for my mom, that's ultimately between them. If she wants to stay with him, that's her cross to bear. It didn't affect my life." I take her face in my hands and tilt her chin up so she's looking at me. "Until you. I lose my mind thinking about you talking to him like that. I thought I'd get over it, but here we are, five months later, and I can't close my eyes at night without thinking of the conversations the two of you had."

"I had no idea it was—"

"I know." I exhale slowly and feel lighter for the

first time in months. "I've read your conversations. I've read them so fucking many times I can't look him in the eye anymore. I know you didn't know it was him. But my point is that if it weren't for his political career, he would never have gone looking for his next mistress on Something Real. He wouldn't have needed to. It's because my father wanted to run for governor that he ended up having an online affair with the only woman I've ever loved."

"I'm so sorry," she says.

I press a hard kiss to her lips. "That's why I'm pretending to be engaged to Sabrina. Because she's been screwed over too, and if our 'engagement' makes the world talk about her wedding dress choices instead of her preference for kinky sex, that's the least I can do."

"But what's in it for you?"

I take a deep breath and thread my fingers through her hair. "More than I ever realized," I whisper.

"How so?"

"It got you back in my life, didn't it?" Then I kiss her in earnest, and she holds me tight as she kisses me back.

CHAPTER FOURTEEN

Liz

HIS SKIN IS HOT under my hands and his mouth hungry as it slants over mine.

When I put my shoes on and decided to come here, I didn't think much further than confronting him, but I couldn't walk away now if I tried.

His erection presses against my stomach, and when my hand skims down the hard planes of his back and south of his waist, I realize he's lost his towel.

Maybe a good person would step away before things went too far, but when it comes to Samuel Bradshaw, I am neither good nor bad. I'm only *his.*

Instead of getting away from his glorious naked body, I scrape my nails down his ass cheeks.

He breaks the kiss and looks down at me, the question in his hot eyes. "What are we doing?"

"I don't know."

"I won't have you walking out my door feeling used again."

I trail my fingers up his back, glorying in the feel of his skin under my fingers. I know I screwed up. I know everything is too complicated for there to be an "us." And yet here we are. "Everything's such a mess. But . . ."

"But?"

Not knowing how to reply, I do what I've wanted to do since he answered the door like that—I press my open mouth to the hard muscle of his shoulder. I work my way down his chest until I taste that sensitive skin under his navel, my hands gripping his ass, and I drop to my knees.

"Rowdy," he growls. His hands are already sliding into my hair, making my sex clench with greedy need.

"Let me." I look up at him through my lashes as I cup his balls in one hand. His head drops back in something so close to surrender it fills me with power.

I wouldn't keep my mouth off this man's dick right now if you paid me.

First, I taste him with my tongue, stroking the underside of his cock while applying slight pressure to his balls. His hips buck and his hands tighten in my hair. I moan my approval and take him into my mouth.

I'm so hungry for him. It's true that I didn't want him to make me the other woman, but now that I know the truth, I realize I was far more worried about losing him forever than I was about what our night at the Conrad said about me.

I suck him hard and take him so deep my eyes water. Whatever happens to us after tonight, I want him to remember something good. Not that shit excuse for pleasure from the other night. Real pleasure. Real satisfaction. *Love.*

I want to remember that I can love someone so much that his pleasure turns me on more than my own. Because in the dark, lonely hours of my months away from him, this kind of love seemed more like a fairytale I'd told myself than a memory.

"Rowdy. Baby." His fists pull my hair and I suck harder, apply a fraction more pressure, and his hips rock into my face with those twitchy, uncontrolled movements that tell me he's lost his control.

I'm so turned on it hurts, and I slide my free hand between my legs, rubbing myself through my panties. The rough lace rubs my swollen clit, and I moan as I suck him.

Sam sees what I'm doing, and the sound that rips from his chest is equal parts pain and pleasure. His orgasm is close. He swells in my mouth and I shift the angle of my hand. I want more. *Need* more. I need *his* fingers, his mouth, his cock filling me so deep the pleasure tears me in half. I force myself to relax my throat to open, and I swallow as he comes.

When his body goes limp and he releases my hair, I draw back and stand.

"Fuck," he murmurs. He traces my lips with his thumb. "This mouth is going to be the death of me."

Then he takes the hand that was just between my legs and sucks two fingers into his mouth.

The act shocks me as much as the pleasure, and I squeeze my legs together. He looks at me through those dark lashes while he examines every inch of my fingers with his tongue, and when he releases them, my breathing is uneven and my legs weaker than before.

He pulls my body against his. Whether he knows it or not, he's holding me up. "Don't do that again," he says.

"What?" I'm not sure which part he didn't like.

"Next time you touch yourself while sucking me off, you'd better be naked so I have a better view."

Sam

I unzip her skirt and let it fall to the floor, then I pull her tank top over her head. She's not wearing a bra underneath, and the sight of her in front of me in nothing but strappy black sandals and a black lace thong takes my breath. Her skin is this flawless ivory, except for the freckles that show up on her shoulders and chest in the summer. Her breasts are pert and perfect, with tight nipples I'm dying to taste.

I'm already too aware of the immediacy of our situation. I won't let this be a repeat of the night at the Conrad, but there's not enough time for what we really need. Soon, she'll need to go home—or back to wherever she's staying tonight. I can't have someone see her leaving my house when I'm supposed to be marrying Sabrina.

Maybe that's why I feel like I need at least an hour for each breast and another for each thigh before settling my mouth on her swollen pussy, where I think I need a day to taste her and suck her and make her scream.

When she touched herself while her mouth was around me . . . hell. I almost came the second she put her hand between her legs and moaned. I didn't plan to let her finish me—not when she was fully dressed and so damn vulnerable. But then she did that, and I was lost.

I cup one of her breasts in my hand and then pinch her nipple. Her lips part and her eyes close. I slip her panties from her hips and hold her hand as she steps out of her shoes. She'd do anything I asked her to right now, and that makes my chest ache as much as it turns me on.

She owns me. And I need her to know it.

"Come with me, Rowdy." I lead her into my bedroom by the hand. Taking her against the wall had been a mistake. I was too desperate for her. Too greedy.

It's not a mistake I intend to repeat tonight.

When I grab a long, soft white rope from my dresser, she bites her lip and eyes it and me alternately. Then, as if something clicks in her mind, her gaze lands on the four-poster bed and her breath leaves her in a rush.

"What are you going to do?" I love that her voice is

laced with excitement and curiosity, not fear.

"I bought this bed after Will and Cally's wedding," I confess. "I didn't like the way those handcuffs cut into your wrists. And with all the posts and support . . ." I grin. "The possibilities."

She worries her bottom lip between her teeth. "You've never tied me up in it."

I cup her face in my hand and turn her to look at me. "I've never tied up anyone else in it either. I couldn't if I wanted to. Not when it was intended for you." I slide my hand down her body, over her breasts and stomach, and finally between her thighs, where she's already wet and swollen. "Do you have any idea how hard it is to go to sleep when I'm lying here thinking of all the things I want to do to you in this bed?"

"It would make a good fantasy."

"*You* make the fantasy. The rest of it is just fun." I toss the rope over the wooden bar that connects the posts at the head of the bed and climb on after it. I lie on my back, adjusting the rope so it's even on both sides.

She climbs into bed after me, straddles my waist, and lets me bind her wrists. And when I tighten the long, free side of the rope, it pulls her arms over her head.

Her eyes go wide, but her breathing's uneven and she's so wet, I can feel it on my stomach. Fuck, I'm already hard again. I want to be inside her. But not yet. I've wanted this for too long.

I pull tighter on the rope, and she has to come further up my chest. "I want you to ride until you come." I lift my hands to her breasts and skim my thumbs over her nipples. She's so gorgeous like this. Arms bound over her head. Exposed to me. Giving me a trust I'm not even sure I deserve.

She tries to scoot backward. When the rope pulls tight, halting her progress, she squeaks. She's too close to the head of the bed to straddle my hips. "I can't reach."

"You can reach just fine. I didn't say I wanted you to ride my cock."

Confusion masks her expression for a second, and then my meaning clicks. "Oh."

"Come here." I slide my hands behind her ass and nudge her closer to my face to make sure she understands what I want.

She moves forward hesitantly, and with every inch, I tighten the ropes so she can't back up. When she gets to my chest, she has to reposition herself so she's up on her knees instead of sitting.

"That's one hell of a view," I murmur as I guide her pussy the rest of the way to my face.

The first taste of her is heaven. Not just how fucking hot her position is, but the sounds she makes as I lick her. I knead her ass as I use my mouth to toy with her clit. Gripping her hips, I pull her close and lick, stroke, suck.

When she squirms like the pleasure and pressure are too much, I slide my tongue inside her, and she screams. As if too self-conscious, she whimpers and tries to back away, but I hold her still, pushing the boundaries of her pleasure until she surrenders to it. She rocks her hips. Once. Twice. A jerky third time. I'm relentless with my tongue and don't back off until she's fucking my face just like I wanted.

I spread her open and trace my finger between her ass cheeks and to the sensitive ring of muscle. She gasps as I touch her there, but I don't enter her, just stroke the sensitive skin. Her shock fades and her muscles release. My ears fill with her moans.

I want to fill her with so much pleasure there's not room for anything else in her mind. I want to claim her. To own her, the way she owns me.

When she's close, I tighten the rope, drawing her arms up as far as she can stretch, and I wrap my lips around her clit and suck.

"Yes. Sam . . . God . . . please." Her hips buck and her body spasms. I love the sound of my name on her lips, repeating like a prayer as she surrenders to the pleasure.

CHAPTER
FIFTEEN

Liz

SAM TENDS TO THE ROPES, loosening them as my body relaxes. I lie down next to him, every muscle turning to mush after being pushed higher and higher over and into the abyss.

When the bindings are gone, he tosses them on the floor and presses kisses around each wrist. My lids are heavy with sleep, but I moan when he rolls over me, resting on his elbows. He's hard, and though I was desperate to have him inside me a couple of minutes ago, now I'm so sated, I just want to go to sleep when I know I should be heading back to Nix's.

"I wish I could have a redo." He tucks a curl behind my ear.

"Seriously?" I yawn. "I wouldn't want you to change anything about that."

He grins. "Good to know, but not what I was talking about."

"A redo for what?"

"Us." He traces the side of my jaw and threads his fingers in my hair. His eyes are sad. "I'd change things. So many things."

I lean my head into his hand. "Me too. I would go back to that night last summer when Connor found me drunk at Brady's, and instead of going home with him I'd call you. I wanted to, but then Connor was there, telling me things I desperately wanted to believe." I swallow. "I wasn't even going home with him. I was going home with the *idea* of him—a guy who'd wanted me from the beginning."

"Did he?"

I shrug. "He said so. He said a lot of sweet things that night."

"Like what?"

I grimace. The memory alone makes me feel guilty. Even though he and Della were broken up, and even though Della had been treating me like shit for months, I broke something in the girlfriend code by going home with Connor. "He said he'd always wanted me, and that every time Della broke up with him, his first thought was that he could be with me now."

Sam's nostrils flare as he draws in a sharp breath. "And you bit, hook, line, and sinker. He's good. I'll give him that."

I frown. "Why do you assume he didn't mean it?"

He shrugs, but there's no anger on his face. In fact, I think this is the first time we've talked about that night without him getting furious. "I didn't say he didn't mean it, but I also think you still give him more credit than he deserves."

"Maybe. Could you tell me what happened between you two? He used to be your friend."

"I don't know why you think Connor is this amazing guy," he says. "You are such a smart girl, but when it comes to him you have blinders on."

"I don't have blinders. Maybe you're the one who's wearing blinders. Especially when it comes to Della." I shake my head and hold my hand up. "I'm sorry. Forget I said that. I don't want to fight. I'm just having trouble imagining what could make you think Connor's so horrible."

"Liz, he slept with you when he was with Della, and when I had feelings for you. He knew I had every intention of getting you to be mine. And he found you at a vulnerable moment, plied you with liquor, fed you his story about Della 'breaking up' with him—"

"She did." Something sinks in my chest, and for the first time, I consider that Connor may have been lying to me that night. "Didn't she?" Would Connor have taken me home if he'd still been with Della and—"You had feelings for me? You . . . *wanted* me?"

He rolls on top of me. "I've wanted you since you were the big-mouthed teenager who would wander around my parents' house without a bra in the middle of the night." He skims his hand down my side then grazes my nipple with his thumb. "You have no idea how many times I jacked off thinking about you. Thinking about the way your nipples poked through your T-shirt." Dipping his head, he sucks one between his lips, then the other. And when he lifts his head again, some of the heat in his eyes has softened to tenderness. "No woman has ever turned me on as much as you do. Never mind the way you could make me laugh like no one else."

I take his face in my hands and lead him down to kiss me. His erection presses into my stomach, and I shift under him, spreading my legs and arching my back until he's positioned exactly where I want him.

"I've wanted you that long too," I whisper as he slides into me.

"You've always been my girl." His eyes lock on mine, and he slowly thrusts deep, then withdraws, then deep again. "Always."

I close the door quietly behind me.

"Jesus!" Nix hisses behind me. "I thought you'd been kidnapped or something."

My plan was to get back here by five a.m. so Nix would never know I'd left. Judging by the fact that she's completely dressed and ready to go at five-oh-two, I guess I should have shot for four instead. "I'm sorry."

She sighs heavily, and guilt courses through me. "Where were you?"

"I . . . woke up early and went for a walk."

She's silent for a beat, studying me with so much disapproval on her face she reminds me of my mother. "If you don't want to tell me, that's fine, but I don't like being lied to. You didn't sleep here all last night, and don't insult me by trying to pretend you did."

"Nix—"

She holds up a hand. "I'm glad you're okay. Let's leave it at that."

"I'm sorry."

"Yeah, well, I need to work." She grabs her purse off the entry table and hoists it onto her shoulder. "I hate him for hurting you," she says without looking at me, "and I'd be the first in line to kick him in the nuts, but at some point you have to take personal responsibility." She crosses her arms and turns to look at me. "You've scraped your heart off the ground and handed it right back to the butcher."

She turns toward the garage and leaves, slamming the door behind her.

I sink to the floor, cradle my head in my hands, and listen to the sound of the garage opening and her car pulling down the drive. She's right. Of course she's right. But she doesn't know the truth about Sam and Sabrina. If I could just tell her . . .

If I told her, it might not change how she feels. So what if Sam and Sabrina's engagement is fake? What does that really mean for us?

My phone buzzes.

Sam: *You left without saying goodbye.*

I start to type a reply, then stop. After everything with River, I'm not a big fan of texts and IMs for communicating. I hit the phone icon and call him instead. He picks up on the first ring.

"If I'd known you were going to run away," he says, "I never would have fallen asleep."

I close my eyes, allowing myself a minute to revel in the sound of his scratchy morning voice. "I didn't make it back before Nix woke up," I say.

"You were supposed to be staying at her place last night?"

"Yeah. She was worried when she woke up and I wasn't here. Once she knew I was safe, she assumed I was with you."

He draws in a breath. "Shit. I know she won't tell anyone, but if she slips—"

"She won't." I tuck the phone between my ear and shoulder and wrap my arms around myself.

"Can you tell her you were with that guy you had at the fundraiser?"

Last night, all I cared about was being with Sam again and knowing that his engagement with Sabrina wasn't real. But this morning, it's painfully obvious that nothing's really changed. "You want me to pretend I spent the night with another man?"

"*Want* isn't really the right word, but it's probably a good idea."

I don't know how to reply. Is it fair to be hurt by that when I knew he planned to continue with the fake engagement?

With every silent second, my stomach sinks further and further until it lands at my feet.

"Well." I swallow. Talk about morning-after awkwardness. We're good at that, Sam and I. "Don't worry about it, okay? You have enough on your plate right now. I'll take care of Nix."

"Is she still there?"

I lift my eyes to the garage door. "She already left to make rounds at the hospital."

"Then come back over. I don't have to be at the bank until nine, and this bed is lonely without you."

"Do you really think that's a good idea? The sun's coming up, and you have nosy neighbors."

He mutters a string of colorful curses. "You're right."

"I need to get back home anyway. I have to work this afternoon."

"Home? Rowdy, *this* is your home."

I bite my lip, because it's not anymore. Until I can be next to Sam without worrying about people seeing us together or stressing over what his family might think, New Hope will never feel like the safe haven a home should. And I'm not sure if that day will ever come.

"Have a good day, Sam."

"You too."

I wait half a beat into the silence where another couple—a *normal* couple—would say *I love you* and hang up the phone. Sam and I never got to be that normal couple. I'm not sure we ever will.

CHAPTER SIXTEEN

Sam

I CAN'T STAY AWAY from her. God help me.

I had plans to go to Brady's with the guys tonight, but I made an excuse about wedding plans and drove to Indianapolis and straight to Lizzy's apartment. She's been dodging my calls all day.

Coming here is risky. Someone could see me. Someone could find out that we used to be together and make a big deal about me visiting her. But if she's not going to talk to me on the phone, I'll get her to talk to me in person.

I climb the stairs to her apartment, and when I reach

her floor, I can hear her laughing on the other side of the door. That sound does something to me. As if there's this little pilot light in my chest, and only Liz can make it burn bright—with her laugh or her smile or her moans.

The door's cracked, so I nudge it open a few more inches without knocking, figuring she's probably on the phone with one of her friends.

Instead, I find her on the couch with that guy she brought to the fundraiser. They're on opposite ends, turned in toward each other and hunched over something. Two beers sit on the coffee table.

That bright warmth in my chest turns cold and sinks into my gut. They make a cozy picture, sitting like that, and maybe he's even a good guy and not some jerk using her for sex and hinting but never promising that it might become more.

That would be you, asshole.

I'm not enlightened enough to direct my anger inward, though, so instead, I clear my throat and set my jaw.

The guy lifts his head, and the smile falls from his face when he sees me. "You have company, Liz."

Liz looks up, but her reaction is the opposite of her friend's. Despite having avoided my calls, she lights up at the sight of me. Her eyes go a little bigger, her smile a little brighter. "What are you doing here?"

I look at him, then back to Liz. "Sabrina wanted me to bring over some files she said you needed for the campaign."

They both stand. Liz shoves her hands into the

pockets of her cut-offs, and her friend looks back and forth between us.

"I'd better get home," he tells Liz. "I promised Mrs. Louise she could bring me dinner."

"Thanks for the beer," she tells him, but it's all she can do to take her eyes off me. *Eat it, loser.*

The guy keeps his face neutral as he passes me, but just as he reaches the door, so low only I can hear, he says, "Congratulations on the engagement."

"Thanks," I mutter, never taking my eyes from Liz. I push the door shut behind him, then stalk toward her.

"I didn't know you were going to be in town tonight."

"I wasn't planning on it." My voice is gruffer than I intend. Seeing her light up like that does something to me. I'm not sure I'm worth that.

She worries her lip between her teeth and stares at my empty hands. "You have files?"

"That was a lie."

"Then why are you here?"

"For you."

Her teeth sink into her bottom lip. She's so damn sexy. She has her hair pulled onto the top of her head in a sloppy bun, and she's in a loose tank and too-short cut-offs. She's beautiful in an effortless way. She was probably wearing this while cleaning the apartment, but I hate that she had *him* here while dressed like that.

"Me?" she says. "Not Sabrina or your dad's campaign or . . ."

"You," I repeat.

She beams then shakes her head, taking the

146

confidence from her smile. "I'm not sure I should, but I like that you came."

"Do you like *him*?"

She frowns. "What? Who? George?" I arch a brow, and she sighs. "Did you really come here to play the irrationally jealous boyfr—" She snaps her mouth shut.

"It's not about jealousy." I shift awkwardly. I'm not good at this touchy-feely crap. I cross the room so I can be closer to her. "Though I'd like to state for the record that if I *were* your boyfriend, I would have punched him for the way he was looking down your shirt when I walked in the door."

She wrinkles her nose. "He was? Really? That's a little . . . tacky."

"He's a guy. He's gonna look." I wrap my arms around her and tug her against me. "But I don't have to like it."

"I don't think it matters what you think about the way George does or doesn't look at me. And it shouldn't matter whether or not I like him."

"It matters."

She looks up at me through her lashes. "Sam . . ." All of that surprise and happiness that lit up her face when I walked in the door is gone. "What is this?"

With a gentle hand, I lift her chin. "This, as in you and me? As in what happened last night?"

She nods.

"Right now, my life is extra complicated."

She steps back, but I wrap my arms around her, trapping her before she can run from what I have to say.

"Let me finish," I whisper into her hair. I make

myself loosen my grip, but damn it, the idea of her running scares the shit out of me.

Liz

Every time I'm with him, I feel this frantic rush in my chest, but I don't know what I'm rushing toward other than heartbreak and misery.

He leans his forehead against mine. "The video, the secrets, Sabrina, my relationship with my father . . . all that shit is complicated as hell. But you and me? That's about as simple as it gets."

"Simple, just sex. Or simple, something more?"

"Are you asking if I'm still in love with you?"

I hold my breath and look into his eyes. Because that's exactly what I need to know and am too afraid to ask.

"I never stopped loving you," he says. "Even when loving you hurt more than I could bear. I didn't have a choice. It would have been easier to choose to stop breathing. Loving you is part of who I am."

Hope rises up, so strong and insistent in my chest that it hurts. After so many months of feeling beaten down, I don't know what to do with hope, and I don't know if my fractured heart is strong enough to hold it. "I love you too."

He kisses my nose, then my eyelids, then each of my

cheeks. When his mouth connects with mine, he sips at my lips like a man determined to savor something precious.

I draw in a ragged breath. "So, I'm just supposed to wait until your pretend engagement ends? Smile and be okay when you hold her for the cameras?"

"Can you go somewhere with me?"

He dodges the question. "Um, sure."

"Good. I'll pull the car around and meet you up front."

It's a cool spring evening, and I pull on a hoodie before I go down to meet him.

The second I climb into his car, I can tell his mood has shifted. He's more serious now. Somber, almost.

He waits for me to buckle, then starts driving.

"Where are we going?"

"I want you to understand something."

I don't ask any more questions, just ride in silence. After five minutes on the interstate, he reaches across the console, takes my hand, and presses my knuckles to his lips.

Something tightens in my chest. He looks so vulnerable.

We exit on the west side of the city, and a few turns later, he's parking in the street of a subdivision of cute craftsman-style homes.

He points to the house across the street. "A couple lives there with their little girl. Lilly. They adopted her a couple of years ago."

The house is dark except for the porch light and the gleam of the TV visible through the big picture window in the front. "Who are they?"

"Lilly's my daughter."

I startle. "Sorry, what?"

"Before Christmas, you asked me about Asia. I told you I didn't talk about it, but that's where I'd go back. If I could have a redo, I'd go back to the first night we slept together and I'd tell you all about Asia. I should have told you the truth then, but instead, you saw me with her and you pushed me away."

"Who is she?"

"Asia is a stripper." He cuts his eyes to me. "We hooked up one night, and she ended up pregnant."

"Sam, I didn't know."

"You said you saw her at my house that night, after our first weekend together. She'd been planning to have an abortion. That night I came home and she was there, and she told me that she'd have the baby. That's what you saw: me grateful that she planned to give me that gift."

"So, she had the baby? You have a child?" How could I not know this? How could he have kept it a secret? Not just from me, but from everyone?

"Not long after that night, she told me that she went ahead and had an abortion after all. She asked me not to contact her. I was so angry I didn't want to anyway. All this time, I thought she'd ended the pregnancy."

We watch the couple stand, and the house goes dark as they shut out the remaining lights. I can tell this is hard for him, so I wait for him to finish his story.

"Christmas morning, she showed up at my house again," Sam says. "This time drunk and rambling about how she'd sold her soul to a blond-haired devil. I think she meant Connor. She said she'd made an agreement to give the child up for adoption and tell me that she'd had an abortion. She changed her story again after she sobered up, but I hired a PI to find out the truth about her pregnancy."

"Connor wouldn't do that." I shake my head, but my chest aches with the possibility. I was the one who told Connor about Asia. I *have to* believe he didn't have anything to do with Sam's child being taken away from him. "He's your friend, and a good guy. How can you believe he'd do something so terrible?"

"He works for my father."

"You think your father put him up to it?"

His brow wrinkles, and I can see all the frustration and hurt he's holding there. He rubs the back of his neck. "That's what I suspect. You don't know what it's like to have politics lead your life, Liz. For years, I've felt my relationship with my dad was one part son, two parts political pawn. My father had an online affair with the woman I love and paid off another woman to keep my child from me—*that* is the kind of world I live in. That's the kind of world Sabrina lives in. Neither of us asked for it."

"Of course not, but you don't *have* to be their pawn, Sam." I shake my head, as if that could slow my spinning mind. Sam has a baby, and his father may have had something to do with him losing her. *I* may have had something to do with him losing her. "Don't let them manipulate you."

He stares out his window silently for a beat. "My

reasons for carrying on with this charade are complicated. I want to help Sabrina because I know what it's like to be fucked over by a parent's political aspirations. And I know it's not fair to you. God knows we've been through enough without piling this on. But it's temporary, and I think it will be worth it."

"I understand," I say softly.

"Do you?" he asks, turning to me. "Because it's not selfless, Liz. I want the attention off the tape for myself too. I don't want the world to know the truth. I'll become a national joke. A spectacle. The scandal of my relationship with Christine would make this exponentially worse than it is now." When I think he's not going to say any more, he says, "Some day, when the right people can pull the right strings and I can meet my daughter, I want to be more than a sex tape. More than an embarrassment."

"You need to talk to your father." *And I need to talk to Connor.* "You deserve to know what happened and what role your family played in it."

He flashes a twisted smile. "I'm not exactly on speaking terms with Mr. Candidate."

"Consider it, Sam. You deserve to know the truth—the whole truth." The words aren't just for him. I'm telling myself too.

CHAPTER SEVENTEEN

Sam

LIZ IS BEAUTIFUL when she sleeps. I didn't sleep much last night—neither of us did. I brought her back to her apartment, undressed her, and took her to bed. When she finally dozed off, her back snuggled against my front, my arm wrapped around her waist, I stayed awake for a long time, trying to make sense of my life.

When she left in December, it seemed hopeless. I couldn't imagine a way that we could make it work after her affair with my father. But now, more difficult than that is trying to imagine a future where she doesn't sleep in my arms every night.

I don't know what we think we're doing, sneaking around when I'm planning a very public wedding to another woman. But the fact is, we're still here together when we both have so much at stake. Everything else seems meaningless against the possibility of losing each other.

I roll out of bed and make coffee. The sun is coming up, and the birds are singing outside the window. I can't stay long. I need to get out of here and head back to New Hope before people are heading to work and I risk someone seeing me.

I pour us each a cup of coffee, heavily doctoring hers with cream and sugar, and I carry the steaming mugs back to the bedroom.

She's rolled over, her arm stretched across my pillow as if she reached for me in her sleep.

I settle the mugs on the bedside table, smooth her hair off her face, and kiss her forehead.

She opens her eyes slowly, her lashes fluttering as if her lids are heavy. "Good morning," she says.

"Good morning." I press a kiss to her lips, tempted to linger. "I have to leave. I brought you coffee."

She pushes up to her elbows and frowns at the clock. "Mornings are evil enough," she grumbles, collapsing back to the bed. "Why make them worse by getting out of bed before seven?"

"Says the woman who used to open her sister's bakery at the crack of dawn."

"Exactly. I speak from experience."

I kiss her frown, but then she moans and slides her hands under the hem of my shirt. Without meaning to, I turn my kiss longer, deeper.

"I have to go," I murmur, even as I climb into bed on top of her.

"Mmm-hmm." She draws her knees up to either side of my hips and yanks off my shirt between kisses. "I don't want you to be late," she says as she releases my cock from my jeans.

I let out a long groan as she strokes the length of me.

"One more time," she says. "I need you one more time."

"If that's what I have to do to change your opinions about mornings, I guess I'll take one for the team."

She giggles, but her laughter is cut off by her moan as I slide into her.

"Damn." I groan. "How can you feel this good every time?" She's slick and hot, and I could die happy inside her.

Twenty minutes later, she's asleep again, a half-smile curving her lips, and I re-dress and head out the door.

"Are you really that selfish?"

I turn to the voice and find Lizzy's neighbor, George. *Fuck.* Probably not good that he knows I stayed the night. "Are you talking to me?"

George rolls his eyes. "Yeah. I am. Do you even care how miserable she's been the last few months? She moved in here and went through every day like a woman serving her sentence. She went to work, came home, slept, ate just enough to function. You did that to her. You're the ex, right?"

I rub the back of my neck. I really don't like George.

"None of this is any of your business."

"I care about her."

"No one asked you to."

"But that's what you do when you're a decent guy—you *care* about the people in your life. Not just yourself. But I don't expect you to know what that's like."

"Listen, dickhead. Back off. You don't know anything about my life or my relationship with Liz."

"I know enough," he mutters. "These walls aren't *that* thick."

Well, fuck. "You're mistaken. Liz and I are friends. That's all." The lie feels like a betrayal to Liz, but there's no way around it.

"You off to meet your fiancée now? Does she know that you have overnight visits with your 'friends'?" I take a step forward, and he holds up a hand. "I don't care about Sabrina or you, frankly, so you don't need to worry about me wrecking that little arrangement for you."

"What do you want?" I ask. His eyes cut to Lizzy's door, and my stomach clenches hard. He wants her, but he can't fucking have her. "Don't meddle in matters you don't understand."

He shakes his head. "She was getting better. Eating more, smiling—not much, but sometimes. She was starting to live her life rather than endure it. But now you're back."

"She's fine."

He nods. "Sure. But I wonder what's going to happen when you break her heart again. You're probably telling her that things aren't serious with Sabrina, that the engagement's a cover-up for the sex-tape scandal, and as soon as the election is over you two can be together again. Am I right?"

I turn on my heel and head to the stairs. I don't like him knowing so many of my secrets, but I especially don't like him waving my promises to Liz in front of my face as proof that I don't deserve her.

Because I'm afraid he's right.

* * *

Liz

"I take back every bad thing I ever said about Sabrina," Grace says. "I might not like her, but I like the company she keeps."

I follow Grace's gaze and see Sam standing in the hallway just outside the call room. My heart does a couple of cartwheels at the sight of him then spins and adds a back handspring for good measure.

Sam's in jeans that are slung low on his hips, and a fitted tee that hugs his biceps. I'm sure he has every woman in the building drooling. Grace certainly is.

He's talking to Sabrina and has a very serious look on his face. Just then, he catches my eye, and his entire expression changes.

"Girl," Grace says, "I hope Sabrina doesn't see him looking at you like that. She'll crucify you."

I force my gaze away from Sam and busy myself stacking fliers for the volunteers. "I don't know what you're talking about."

"Mmm-hmm. Just watch yourself. I don't know what kind of complicated love triangle you three are involved in, but it would be messy if it came out. Did you see we're up in the polls this morning? Up. Like, higher than pre-sex-tape numbers."

I swallow. "I saw that. Everyone loves a love story, I guess."

"And yet he's heading over here," she says, walking away before I can reply.

Sure enough, seconds later, I sense him behind me.

"May I have a word with you, Miss Thompson?"

"Sure." I paste on a professional smile and avoid Grace's gaze as I follow Sam out of the call center and into an empty office in the back hallway.

"What do you need?" I sound nervous. I *am* nervous.

He locks the door behind me and pulls the blinds on the big windows separating the room from the hallway.

He turns back to me, his eyes hot, intense, and when he leans in to kiss me, I don't try to stop him. I let his lips sweep against mine. My eyes close as I inhale his scent and allow myself just for a minute to live in this moment.

My entire body buzzes with adrenaline. We shouldn't be doing this here. We probably shouldn't be doing this at all, but I don't just miss him when we're apart. I miss him when he's next to Sabrina. He can be in the room with me, but when Sabrina's by his side and he's acting as if she is his girl, I feel more alone than I have in my whole life.

Maybe it's masochistic to revel in these moments I get alone with him, but only in the way it's masochistic to breathe the little air in the room when suffocation is inevitable.

"You know what this room reminds me of?" he asks.

I never thought of it until being in here with him now, but it's very similar to the conference room where we snuck away at that wedding our first night together. "What?"

He stalks toward me, and I back up until my thighs hit the edge of the conference table. "That wedding." He lifts me onto the table and steps between my legs. "I met you in that conference room, and you told me your rules. Do you remember your rules?"

"I said sex couldn't change things between us. And you said . . ."

"Sex changes everything." He brushes his knuckles across my breasts. My nipples tighten under the lace of my bra. He finds them and pinches them through the fabric.

I have to bite my lip. We can't make any noise. There are probably two dozen people at headquarters tonight, and if any one of them finds out what we're doing in here, we'll both be in trouble.

He cups my breast in his hand as his mouth skims down along the side of my neck and he nibbles at the juncture of my neck and shoulder. When he opens his mouth against the skin and sucks, I gasp. He groans softly, his fingertips sliding over my stomach until his hand settles between my parted legs, cupping me through my jeans.

"I told you you'd never be able to look at me without thinking of the things I did to you."

I swallow. This is insane. "You were right."

"What was the other rule?" His fingers dance against me with just enough pressure to make me desperate for more.

"We couldn't tell anyone."

He grins. "Yeah, I screwed that one up when Connor came to your place. I wanted him to know you'd spent the night with me. I wanted him to know you were mine." He slides his hands under my shirt and slips his fingers into the waistband of my jeans.

"What are you doing?" I whisper.

"Something I wanted to do in the conference room that night."

"What's that?"

"Put my face between your legs," he says. "Taste you."

"You did that later," I say. "Don't you remember the shower?"

His touch is so light it's making me crazy. I want him to rub hard against my jeans and give me what I need. If we were somewhere else, anywhere else, I would press into him, tell him what I want, but the voices of other staffers in the hall remind me there's only a locked door between us and disaster.

"I remember the shower," he says with an appreciative groan. "But in the shower, there wasn't the risk of getting caught. And I love how wet you get when you think we might get caught. Let me taste that."

He unbuttons my jeans and tugs them and my panties from my hips, throwing them to the floor before I can even decide if I can do this.

Then he's sinking to his knees and—"Sam," I hiss. But God, his mouth is hot and open against me, and his lips . . . "Just . . . *oh, God.*"

He didn't shave today, and his stubble scrapes the tender skin of my inner thighs, contrasting sharply with the soft sweep of his tongue over my clit. He slides his hands under my ass and pulls me against his face. I have to lean back on one hand to steady myself, but the other goes to his hair. I take a fistful as my hips lift off the table, climbing toward pleasure without my consent.

He looks up at me through thick lashes as he slides his finger inside me for the first time. My body instantly squeezes around him, and I pull back, resisting the pleasure that steals my control.

"Don't. Don't quit on me now," he whispers. "I'm not leaving this room until I've made you come." As he slides another finger inside me to join the first, he lowers his lips to my clit and sucks.

Closing my eyes, I throw my head back and surrender to his lips and tongue on my clit, his fingers fucking me and making me crave something more, something deeper. Climbing, climbing, until—"Stop."

I stumble back onto the table, away from his mouth and touch.

When he looks at me, his honey eyes have gone dark. "Where do you think you're going?"

My breathing is shallow and ragged, and my body is completely unsatisfied. I swallow hard. "I was afraid I might scream."

He wraps an arm around my waist and pulls me against him, guiding me off the table and to my feet. My breasts press against his chest, and his erection presses into my stomach through his jeans.

He lets out a gravelly moan. "We can't have that."

"Sorry."

He cocks a brow. "You think I'm done with you?" He skims his lips down my neck, that rough stubble scraping my skin. "You can scream later, but right now I need you to come quietly. Turn around."

The little piece of my brain that had me backing away from him moments again disintegrates as he spins me in his arms and bends me over the table. His hand snakes up my shirt, tracing the length of my spine down to my ass, all the way to my center. His cock nudges my entrance, and I arch my back instinctively to give him the right angle.

"You make me lose my mind," he whispers.

He places his fingers over my mouth in a reminder of our need for silence. Then he slides inside me, and when I want to scream, I bite instead, tasting the salt of his flesh as he drives into me from behind.

He keeps one hand on my hip, guiding me with each thrust. I look over my shoulder, and he's watching us where are bodies are joined.

His hand loosens its hold, and I draw his finger between my lips, tasting, biting, sucking. He thrusts harder and I meet him, stroke for stroke until he pulls his hand from my mouth and finds my clit with his wet fingers.

I bite down on my own arm to keep from crying out as my orgasm slams into me. Seconds later, he comes with a violent thrust.

I rest my head on my forearms, catching my breath, and feel him withdraw.

When I turn back around he's zipping his jeans, his lips twisted into a mischievous grin.

I find my jeans and hurry into them. I'm being reckless. I'd probably lose my job if Sabrina knew what we just did. "Are you done with me now?"

The grin falls away, and he cups my face in his hands. "I could never be done with you, Rowdy."

CHAPTER EIGHTEEN

Liz

I DON'T WANT to be watching as Sabrina Guy and Samuel Bradshaw choose an engagement ring. Unfortunately, the event has been picked up by one of the national morning talk shows, and watching has been deemed relevant to my job. So here I sit in a room with half a dozen other staffers watching as cameras follow the "couple" into a jewelry store, as if their choice of ring were as important to our talking points as Christine's position on matters of foreign policy.

Just yesterday, Sam was stripping me in the conference room. Today he's on national television, buying another woman a ring. Sleeping with him while he's pretending to be engaged to my boss's daughter is worse than risky. It's foolish.

Sam looks handsome this morning. I'm sure someone told him exactly what to wear and exactly how much to spend and exactly how close he's supposed to be to Sabrina. I'm sure someone told him how much he's supposed to smile, practiced the best way for him to look thoughtful, and happy, and relieved that his secret romance is out there in the world. But none of that changes the fact that my heart aches when I see him on the TV screen, grinning at another woman.

None of that changes the fact that I still wish that smile were being directed at me.

"Thank you so much for letting us tag along this morning," the journalist says. They're in a limo in front of Tiffany's in New York City. "I imagine you two have had quite a week."

Sam and Sabrina exchange a look, and he chuckles softly.

"You can say that again," Sabrina says. She's wearing a blue dress—something modest and perfectly cut for her figure. She looks sexy and classy all at once. I'm sure the idea was to make it clear that this isn't some floozy wild-child daughter of a politician. Her outfit is all about understated sexiness.

"So have you two looked at rings before?" the journalist asks.

"We have," Sabrina says. She grins at Sam. "He's got good taste, so I have no doubt he would have picked out something I loved."

"But she should have exactly what she wants," Sam says. "Which brings us here."

I can't tear my eyes from the screen as they go into the store, his arms wrapped around her shoulders.

"You're staring," Grace says under her breath.

"I'm watching," I whisper. "Like everyone else here."

"*We* are watching. *You* are mooning. Interesting how you and Sam disappeared at the same time yesterday. Something you want to tell me?"

"He, um, wanted some advice about a surprise for Sabrina."

"Uh-huh." Grace quirks a brow, but she's a good enough friend not to point out that I'm a shitty liar.

The room quiets, and I know before I turn around that Governor Guy has walked in. We all turn to face her.

"Look at you!" she calls across the small sea of volunteers. "Making a difference one phone call at a time!" The volunteers and staffers all cheer, and the governor turns her gaze to me. "Would you follow me, Liz?"

My pulse kicks up a notch. Is this about what happened yesterday? Does someone know about Sam and me? Did they tell her?

Since I started here, I've been worried that Christine would learn the real reason Mr. Bradshaw recommended me for the position, and the rare times she does acknowledge my existence I'm always waiting for the other shoe to drop.

But now I'm sleeping with her daughter's fiancé and

I'm not just waiting for the other shoe to drop, I'm waiting for the whole damn shoe store. Of course, Christine knows better than anyone that Sam and Sabrina's story is a lie.

I nod and follow her out of the room and to her office.

"You can close that door," she says when we step inside.

"Okay." I shut the door behind me and paste on my best "I'm here to help" face. "What can I do for you?"

"Have a seat." She lowers herself into her chair and offers me an apologetic smile as I follow her lead. "How are you holding up?"

"What do you mean?"

She straightens the papers on her desk. "You and Sam were together before you moved here to take this job. How are you handling the media blitz on his private affair with my daughter?"

Private affair with you, *you mean.* Not that I have the balls to say that. "I . . . well . . ." I swallow hard because the numbness that has served me so well today is faltering, and I want to cry. Why is it that I can take one hit after another and stand strong, but the second someone shows me an ounce of compassion, I lose my shit?

"Oh, Liz. I didn't realize you still had feelings for him. I'm so sorry."

I shrug. It's safer than speaking.

"Well, I apologize on Sabrina's behalf. I know she wouldn't have wanted you to find out like this. But I'm sure you understand why they were so quiet about their

167

relationship."

"Of course."

"Why don't you take the rest of the day off? You don't need to stand around and watch the man you once loved pick out a ring for his fiancée on national television. Go home, or go shopping. Something to get your mind off everything."

I shake my head. "This week might be one of the most important for the campaign."

She holds up her hand. "You don't have to prove your work ethic to me. I've seen it."

I'm not sure when. She's rarely ever here. "We're back up in the polls," I say. "I want to help—"

"Take the day. It's not an offer; it's an order. We'll be here tomorrow."

"Yes, ma'am." It's clear Christine isn't the hugging kind, but I'm not sure if I should shake her hand or just leave, so I nod and make my way out the door.

* * *

When I hit the sidewalk outside of headquarters, Connor's leaning against the building.

"Liz." He stands. "Can we talk?"

I nod slowly and close the door behind me. "Is everything okay?"

He falls into step beside me and drags a hand through his mop of blond hair. He looks tired. Red eyes, pale skin, and sagging shoulders. "Yes. No. I don't know. Della's threatening divorce."

"Okay." I wrap my arms around my middle and throw a glance back toward headquarters. I don't like to imagine what Sam would think of this conversation. Last time Della left Connor, Connor talked me into going home with him. That's not a mistake I intend on making again, even if I was tempted. "But why are you here, Connor?"

He flinches. "There was a time that we were good enough friends to talk when one of us had a broken heart."

"That was before you took me home with you and convinced me you and Della were through." I put it out there as a challenge.

He holds up a hand. "I'm not here to fight. Honestly, I'm not even here about Della. I'm here to warn you." His voice is low, dramatically ominous.

"Warn me? About what?"

"I don't want to see you hurt. Whatever you might think of me, I care about you. A lot. And I hate seeing you be so reckless."

"I don't understand what you think might hurt me."

He looks to headquarters then back to me. "You don't want to fuck with Sabrina. You think Della is possessive, but you've never seen Sabrina in action."

"I don't know what you're talking about."

"I saw you at Sam's on Monday night."

My steps falter but I force myself to keep moving forward. "I didn't stay with him. I went to his house to drop something off." Stupidest possible excuse. Why would I park my car at Brady's and walk to Sam's?

Why would I drop off anything to him at that hour?

"Stay away from him. Sabrina gets what Sabrina wants. He's marrying her. Whatever you've made yourself believe, whatever he's told you, you need to understand that this wedding is going to happen."

"Of course it is." My stomach flip-flops, though, because his eyes hold a warning. How much of the truth does Connor know? I swallow. "I actually needed to talk to you."

He cocks his head at me. "About what?"

I take a breath. It's hard to ask a question when you don't want to know the answer. "Were you behind the thing with Asia and the baby? Did his dad have you bribe her?"

This time it's Connor's steps that falter. "I can't talk about that, Liz. The less you know, the better."

"I'm the one who told you her name. It's my fault, isn't it?"

He shakes his head and pulls me into an alley, looking over each shoulder before looking back to me. "Don't do this. You are meddling into matters you should stay far away from. Just stay away from Sam and forget you know anything about Asia."

He doesn't just look tired and stressed. He looks scared. "What do you know that you aren't telling me, Con?"

He shakes his head. "I shouldn't be here. I'm gonna go." He turns in the opposite direction. "Take care of yourself, Liz."

CHAPTER NINETEEN

Liz
One year ago . . .

I HAND MY NIECE back to my sister, and the second she leaves my arms, part of me feels empty. The twins are beautiful. I imagined I'd have twins one day. When we were kids, Hanna and I always talked about how we would grow up and buy houses next door to each other, get married at the same time, and get pregnant at the same time. Of course we'd both have twins—we couldn't imagine it any other way—and we'd raise the four like siblings.

Intellectually, I knew that wasn't going to be our

future. What are the chances of it working out like that, right? But it still hurts, and not because I don't want Hanna to have everything she has. It's just that I want to have it too.

For a moment I'm tempted to ask for Sophie back. Since there are two of them, it would be easy enough to stay at Hanna and Nate's all night long and always be holding one baby. After the twins were born, I stayed over here for a couple of nights. I would get up with them in the middle of the night, and I would rock one twin while Hanna fed the other. In the darkness, with a warm baby snuggled against my chest, I would imagine they were mine. Sleep deprivation and midnight feedings didn't seem bad to me. Instead, they seemed like this wild adventure that I wanted desperately.

Hanna holds out her hand so I can inspect her new engagement ring. It glitters in the light, and the sight of it on her finger makes something pull hard in my chest.

"Congratulations." My throat is thick with my tears. I force in a ragged breath, and then another, but it's not enough to fill the emptiness inside me. This is my sister. My twin. My other half. And she has a life. She has her babies and now her fiancé. She has her business. It's as if my life has been paused since we graduated from college, and she's been carrying on with hers.

"Are you okay?" Hanna bites her lower lip, her brow wrinkling with worry.

"I'm fine. I'm just so happy for you." I curl my lips and hope it resembles a smile. I won't ruin this night for her by letting her discover my internal pity party.

"Della wanted to meet for drinks at Brady's tonight. We have some business stuff to discuss. You won't be upset if I leave, will you?"

"Of course not." Hanna wraps her arms around me and squeezes tight. "Tell the wench I said hi."

I feel a little guilty for the lie. But not much. I'd rather lie and get out of here than risk her seeing just how sorry I'm feeling for myself. If Hanna knew how lonely I've felt lately, it would steal part of her joy. And she deserves to be happy, more than anyone I know.

I say my goodbyes and head for the door. In the front room, Asher has Maggie against the wall, his hands buried in her hair, his mouth pressed against hers. They're always like that, even after all this time together. I'm beginning to think they'll never change, and dang, wouldn't that be nice?

I sneak past before they can see me and go straight to my car.

When I get to Brady's, I'm surprised to see the place is pretty quiet. Then again, Sinclair is out for the spring, and business slows down when summer comes.

I sidle up to the bar, and Brady grins at me. "If it isn't my favorite blonde."

"And if it isn't my favorite barkeep."

He pulls out two shot glasses and fills them both with tequila. I grab one, and he takes the other. "I hear your sister got engaged tonight."

I cock a brow, then shoot back my tequila before answering. "News travels fast."

"It's already up on that new gossip site. The *Tattler*?"

"Yeah, I'm familiar with it."

He refills my tequila. "Yeah, I figured I'd be seeing you tonight. And I figured you'd need a drink."

"I'm that predictable, huh?"

"You're human. Don't beat yourself up over it."

"What's wrong with me?" I study the amber liquid, frowning. "I've never had a serious relationship. I have no prospects on the horizon. And I have no idea what I want to do with my life."

"You've got a prospect right here. I can't buy you no fancy ring, but I'd treat you real good." He grins, and the skin around his eyes wrinkles. Brady's handsome, and kind, and about thirty or forty years too old for me. "And what do you mean, you don't know what you want to do with your life? You've got that business with Della. The preschool does well, doesn't it?"

I sigh, my shoulders sagging. "I hate it. I just haven't wanted to tell anybody. I feel like a failure."

"Do you hate that your business partner is a bitch? Or do you hate running a preschool?"

"Both," I admit. I've come here after work more than once. Brady has heard his fair share of Della horror stories. I used to think she was my friend, but now I think that we just traveled in the same circles and assumed we were close. She is horrible to me. Just last week, I screwed up someone's monthly tuition bill and I overheard her talking to one of the parents as she tried to clear it up. *"There are people like me, who teach preschool because they love children. And then there are people who teach preschool because they aren't smart enough to teach anything else."*

Their laughter hurt so much, I wanted to walk out and hide. But I pretended I didn't hear and finished out the day.

"Life's too short to do something you hate," Brady says.

"I would quit if I had any idea of what to do with myself." And, with that depressing thought, I shoot back the second dose of tequila. Tonight, I'm thinking of the shots as doses. Doses of medicine. Doses of happiness in a little glass. Doses of sanity.

"You driving tonight?" He extends his hand, palm up. It's not really a question.

I dig my keys from my purse and plop them into Brady's hand. "I'll walk home if it means you give me another."

He pockets my keys and refills my glass.

"You know why I'm so jealous of Hanna?" I ask.

"I'll bite," Brady says.

"Nate has wanted her all along. Even when he didn't think he wanted anyone, Nate wanted Hanna."

"Not sure it was that simple," Brady says.

"I mean that she'll never have to feel like he settled for her. He would've moved mountains to be with her. He would've let her go and have been miserable without her if that's what he needed to do to make her happy. And she didn't have just one, but two guys who loved her. I want a little taste of that."

Brady shakes his head and sighs before refilling my glass. I don't even remember drinking that last shot, but here I am with a new one. "I still think you're oversimplifying it. Nate's not perfect. No man is."

"Maybe that's my problem. Maybe I'm looking for the perfect guy. And what I really need to be looking for is the guy who's perfect for me. The one who would move mountains to be with me."

Brady grunts. "That's an awful lot of self-pity there, champ."

I sigh. "I know. I'm the worst."

"Nah. We're all entitled to a pity party from time to time." He moves down the bar to help another customer.

"Hey," someone says behind me.

I turn and see Connor standing behind the stool next to mine, his face drawn with worry, his fingers gripping the top of the seat. "You mind if I join you?"

"Go ahead." My words are starting to slur a little. Good old tequila, doing its thing. I throw back the next shot as Connor settles in next to me.

"I see your life is shit, too," Connor says.

I cut my eyes to him. "So, how much of that conversation did you just overhear?"

He avoids my gaze and waves a hand at Brady. "Enough to know that what they say is true. The thing that you want is right in front of you, and you don't even know it."

I blink at him, and my vision clears and the two Connors merge into one. Maybe I should slow it down on the booze. It sure seems as if Connor is coming on to me. "Listen . . ."

Connor hangs his head, and Brady slides a tall stout in front of him then leaves us again. "Forget I said anything," Connor says.

"You're with Della," I remind him. If I were sober, I wouldn't say it. If I were sober, I wouldn't be ballsy enough to think that my business partner's long-term boyfriend was coming on to me. But I'm not sober. Even though we agreed to part as friends after that one night together at Notre Dame, I've always felt as if Connor's carried a torch for me.

"No, I'm not." Connor drags a hand through his sloppy blond hair. "She broke up with me."

"Again?"

He looks over his shoulder before answering. "She does this all the fucking time. I don't give her what she wants, and she breaks up with me. I don't give her enough attention, and she breaks up with me. I look too long at an attractive woman on the street, and she breaks up with me."

"So you're not really broken up. She's just throwing a little fit."

"I don't know. She packed her bags, and she left. Tomorrow she'll probably want to get back together."

He looks over his shoulder again, and this time I follow his gaze to a redhead in a booth. She reminds me of someone but I can't place her. When Connor turns back to me, I can see the exhaustion in his eyes.

"I'm done," he says. "I can't take the constant emotional manipulation anymore. She doesn't want to be with me. She wants somebody who will do her bidding. She wants somebody who will tell her she's beautiful every day and who she can insult in return."

"But you love her."

Connor exhales slowly. Once again, he looks over

his shoulder, but I'm not sure if he's looking at the redhead or just buying time to answer. He takes a long drink of his beer. "That's true. But not all love is created equal. I keep hoping she'll love me desperately, but she doesn't."

"What about you? Do you love *her* desperately?"

"Touché." He attempts a smile, but it's forced. The room spins. "I guess there's only one girl I've ever really felt that way about."

Oh, shit. "Connor . . ."

"I spent a lot of years pretending that I don't want you, Liz." Brady's still at the other end of the bar, but he says the words quietly so only I can hear. He cocks his head at me and his mop of hair flops over one eye. "I can't be with Della. It's not fair to her."

"Why not?"

"Because the first thing I think every time she breaks up with me is, maybe I can be with Liz now."

The room spins a little, like it does in the movies when the boy says something to the girl and it's so sweet and it's so special that the camera has to do a little semicircle.

"I know you've only ever wanted friendship from me," he says. "But I swear I'd treat you like a queen."

"Connor . . ."

He scoots forward on his stool and dips his head as if he's going to kiss me right here and now.

I stop him with a finger to his lips.

The redhead scoots out of her booth and smirks at us as she walks to the door.

"I don't want to be alone tonight," Connor says.

"Come home with me?"

CHAPTER TWENTY

Sam

ONE HOTEL ROOM. One giant bed. Two people who have no interest in sleeping together.

"I can sleep on the couch," Sabrina says.

I shake my head. "Take the bed. I don't mind."

"You could join me." She holds up a hand as if signaling me to stop my train of thought. "Not like that. I mean there's enough room for both of us."

"I don't mind the couch."

She smiles. "You're a true gentleman. Mind if I take a soak?" She points over her shoulder toward the marble-tiled bathroom. It's beautiful and reminds me of the hotel in Chicago where I took Liz last December. The bathtub where she slid down my cock without anything between us, her arms wrapped around my neck.

"Take your time."

I'm exhausted. My jaw hurts from smiling all day, from pretending to be madly in love while dropping a small fortune on that ridiculous ring. But mostly, I'm sick of pretending. And this is just the beginning. I'm starting to question my decision to go all in on this charade, but I really do feel for Sabrina. She's the victim in this.

As soon as the bathroom door clicks closed behind her, I pour myself a drink from the mini-bar and sink into the couch with my phone.

The phone rings once before Liz picks up. "Hello?" Her voice is a little sleep roughened.

"Did I wake you?"

She yawns. "I fell asleep on the couch. I haven't been getting much sleep lately. Trying to catch up."

"I guess it's good I'm not home tonight then," I say. "Because I'm so selfish, I'd keep you up all night. Again. How was your day?"

"Well, I got sent home from work. Governor Guy realized that your relationship with her daughter must be hard on me and told me to take the day off."

"Shit. I didn't think about that. You didn't let on that you knew anything, did you?"

"Of course not. What was I going to do? Look her in the eye and tell her I know she and I have a penchant for the same kind of sex? I'll pass on that awkward conversation, thanks. I don't think I want to bond with her over our shared bedroom partners or techniques."

I chuckle. "You think your *techniques* are like hers, huh?"

"I try not to think about it, but hey, I did see the video."

"First of all, I'd like to think *my* techniques have improved since then, but . . ." My gaze drifts to the bathroom door. It's still closed, and there's no way Sabrina can hear me over the loud hum of the jetted tub. "It's not the same with you, Rowdy."

"How so? Are you trying to tell me I'm good in bed?"

"Good doesn't begin to cover it." I close my eyes and picture her tied to my bed, her arms extended above her head, breasts rising and falling with her breath, lips parted as if her body is too full of pleasure and she needs to give it a place to escape. "Have you ever had sex with someone you didn't love?"

She's quiet for a minute. "You know the answer to that."

"Ah, Connor. Fucker. He should never have slept with you."

"One might say the same thing about Christine Guy and you," she says softly.

"I'm sure Sabrina would agree."

She sighs. "No doubt. I tend to forget how shitty this situation must be for her."

"Thank you for understanding." I take a long drink of my scotch. Liz and I are in limbo. My situation has given us an excuse to be together in that it prevents us from really being together. There are no tough decisions about whether or not I can have her in my life after what happened with my dad, because she can't be in any real way. At least not yet. Maybe I needed that excuse at first, but I don't now. We might have to fight for this, but she's worth it. "Liz?"

"Yeah?"

"It's different with you. Not just better in terms of getting off and feeling good. Better in all ways. Fuller. I didn't think it could get any better than that first night with you, but it does. Every time."

"It's the same for me."

I'm still in love with you. I never stopped. I will always *love you.* The words stall on my tongue.

I hear water running on the other end of the phone. "Are you taking a bath?"

"Yep. I have a big glass of wine, plenty of hot water, and no plans for the rest of the day. A bath sounds like as good a plan as any."

"George isn't coming over to keep you company?"

"He's just a friend."

I force my jaw to unlock. I'm the one who brought him up. It's not fair for me to get pissed. "He wants more."

Water sloshes on the other end of the line. She's climbing into the tub. "I know, but he also knows that I'm still hung up on someone else."

I want her to be more than *hung up* on me. I want her to be so hopelessly in love that she'll give this a chance, despite the odds being stacked against us. Maybe with time. "Are you in the tub?"

"I even have bubbles," she says.

"I miss taking baths with you. What exactly do you do when you're in the water alone?"

"Are you asking me if I'm about to touch myself?"

My cock strains against the fly of my pants. It's so easy to imagine her in a bath of bubbles, her hand between her legs. "No, I'm telling you I want you to touch yourself."

She draws in a breath. "Oh."

"You'd be doing me a big favor. See, I'd do it myself if I wasn't seven hundred miles away."

"So, it'd be more like a favor for a friend?"

"The best kind of favor."

"If you put it that way . . ."

"Start at your breasts. I want you to touch your nipples. Are they hard?"

She draws in a breath. "Yeah."

"Play with them for me. Roll them between your fingers." The sound of her gasp has me shifting uncomfortably again. I check the bathroom door, but it's still closed and the jets are still going.

"God," she moans, dragging out the word. "Are you sure you can't fly home tonight? I'd pick you up at the airport, maybe find a dark alley so we didn't have to wait until we got back to my place."

"Don't distract me," I growl. "Are you ready for more?"

"More than I can have with you in New York City."

I close my eyes. Flying home and being with Liz is so much more appealing than sleeping on this couch. "Put your hand between your legs and find your clit."

She inhales, then slowly releases her breath. Just the sound of her breathing over the phone is enough to make my dick ache. "Good girl. Now slide a finger inside yourself while you rub your clit with your palm."

"Sam." There's a desperate pitch to her voice, and I know my words are doing as much for her as her touch.

"Keep going. I need to hear you breathe. I want to hear you moan."

I hear the sound of sloshing water, then her moan. Her breathing changes, shallows, becomes more labored.

"Add a second finger."

"But—"

"Imagine I'm there watching you. Imagine I'm standing by the tub and I'm watching you finger-fuck yourself. Put on a show for me, Rowdy."

She moans. "I . . . *God* . . ."

"Move slowly. You don't want it to end. Imagine I'm watching you and you want to make it last." That's where I want to be. Right there, watching her get herself off, watching the pleasure on her face as I whisper dirty words in her ear. She'd fist my dick in her hand and—

My ears fill with the sounds of her orgasm, sweet little pants and moans that about make me come in my jeans without even touching my dick. I'm gonna need to do something about this soon, but the idea of jacking off with Sabrina in the same room doesn't sit well.

"Wow." She releases a long, relaxed sigh. "Well, and to think I was prepared to be sexless until I saw you again."

"No need for that," I murmur, refilling my scotch.

"You can use the bathroom now," Sabrina says.

I lift my head. Sabrina is standing in front of me in a robe, a towel wrapped around her head. I'm surprised I didn't notice the jets turn off. Then again, I was more than a little distracted.

"Who's that?" Liz asks.

I swallow. The whole roommate situation would have been better addressed in the first half of this conversation. "It's Sabrina."

Liz

I feel as if he's punched me, but I force myself to take a breath and stay calm. "What is Sabrina doing in your room?"

"Can I call you back?" Sam asks.

I flinch and bite down on my bottom lip to keep from speaking. He's not mine. I have no claim to him. This is just . . . I don't even know what this is, other than hopeless. "No need."

"I will call you back," he says firmly.

Say my name. I wish he would say my name. "Sure. Whatever works is fine." I hang up before he can, but being the one to end the call doesn't provide me with the satisfaction I'm looking for.

I toss my phone across the room and drain the tub

then my wine. So much for a relaxing evening.

I pull on my robe, and I'm halfway to the kitchen to refill my glass when I hear the phone ring. I could ignore it. He'd just talked me to the best solo orgasm I've had in my life and I'd hardly recovered when Sabrina was suddenly there.

I'm being irrational. Of course she's there. That's why he's in New York, right? But why is she in his room?

I can't resist getting the answers I need, so I run to the bathroom to grab the phone, answering it right before it would go to voicemail. "Hello."

"Sorry about that. I didn't realize Sabrina had gotten out of the tub."

Out of the tub. So. Fucking. Intimate. "I wonder if she's as innocent in all of this as you think."

"What's that supposed to mean?"

"Come on. You're sharing a room? You're in New York with her for the second time *this week*, parading around like a happy couple."

"That was kind of the deal, Liz. I thought you understood."

"It's just . . ." I have no idea how to articulate what I'm feeling, probably because I can't seem to identify the emotions for myself. Jealousy and envy, because his family would welcome her with open arms, but also something else. Something about this whole arrangement seems off. I don't trust her.

"It's just what?" He sighs, and I hear a knocking on his side of the line.

"It feels convenient."

"The press will find out if we sleep in separate rooms," he says. "We figured it wouldn't be a big deal to share a room tonight."

That would have been nice to know *before* he played phone-sex operator. "Connor warned me about her. I think you should be careful."

"Connor? Why were you talking to my asshole brother-in-law about Sabrina?"

"He was trying to warn me," I say too loudly. I don't want to fight, and I've already said too much. Bringing up Connor is bound to make Sam upset, and Sabrina's conveniently there, trying to get his attention. "I thought you were alone." I even imagined him in bed, stroking his cock as he said those things to me. The idea was half of what got me off so quickly. "You don't need to stay on the phone with me. Go ahead and go. Sleep well." *With Sabrina.*

"I'm not sleeping with her." He gives a heavy sigh, as if he's completely exasperated. With me, or the situation?

"Is it really my business if you are?" I shout. I throw my hand over my mouth and squeeze my eyes shut. I sound crazed and irrational.

"It is," Sam says. "It's your business because *you're* the one I love." His sigh fills the line again. "Tell me what you want me to do. If you want me to come home tonight, I'll do it. I'll find a way. I'll find an excuse to give the press. I can't stand the idea of hurting you. Tell me what you want me to do."

But I can't have what I want when what I want is for him to leave without me having to tell him. "Sleep well,

Sam. I'll see you . . ." When? Why? "I'll see you when I see you."

CHAPTER
TWENTY-ONE

Sam

"I LOVE YOU," I whisper, but Liz has already disconnected the call. I slam my fist into the door, and pain shoots up my arm. *Fuck.* I need a drink.

When I get out of the bathroom, Sabrina's dressed in a silky robe and her hair is dry.

"Who was on the phone?" she asks.

I rub the back of my neck. I'm not sure it's fair to keep my relationship a secret from Sabrina, but I don't exactly want to share either. "A friend."

She crosses her arms and lifts her chin. "Let me guess—Elizabeth Thompson?"

"Yeah."

"You trust her?"

Well, there's a question. Five months ago, I would have said no, but I never would have admitted the truth about the video to her if I believed she'd hurt Christine or me with it. "Yeah, I do."

"You told her the truth?"

"She figured it out on her own."

She studies me for a few beats then shakes her head. "I don't know about you, but this room is already feeling claustrophobic. I'm going to get dressed and head down to the bar. Want to join me?"

I'd rather let her go to the bar while I call Liz back, but I'm pretty sure Liz has heard enough from me for one night. "Sure. I could use a drink." I close my eyes and hear Liz saying, *I'll see you when I see you.* "Or twelve."

Liz

Instead of refilling my wine, I get dressed, pull my hair into a ponytail, and drive to New Hope. When I get to town, I pull over and rest my head on the wheel. It's nearly ten. I know Hanna would be thrilled to see me, but she doesn't know what's going on between Sam and me, and I don't think Sam would want me to tell her. He doesn't want me to tell anyone.

SOMETHING REAL

I text Nix.

Liz: *Where are you?*

Nix: *I'm home. What's going on?*

I pull back onto the road and go straight to her place. I haven't talked to her since she stormed out after my night with Sam. I know Sam wants me to lie to her, but I won't do that. It's hard enough to keep the truth from Hanna. I need someone to talk to, and since Nix already knows more than anyone else, she's my best bet.

Nix came to New Hope a couple of years ago and recently bought and renovated a big house in town.

I love the house—a Cape Cod in a sunny yellow with a wraparound porch—and when I pull into the drive, I take a minute to look at it. It's the kind of house that screams *home*. I can imagine opening a bottle of wine and spending my night bitching to her about my relationship—or lack thereof—with Sam.

I knock on the door, and when a guy opens it, I have to do a double take.

Max is standing in front of me. Shirtless. Unbuttoned jeans hanging on his hips. His eyes go wide, and then he grins and holds up a wad of bills. "You are not the pizza delivery guy."

"No. I'm not."

Lifting onto my toes, I peek over his shoulder and see Nix setting her dining room table in her T-shirt. And nothing else.

Wow. Awkward.

I raise a brow. "So, you and Nix?"

"Um. I think I'd rather let her answer that?" He turns around. "Lizzy's here."

The silverware clatters from Nix's hands and onto the table. "You didn't text back."

I look to Max and then Nix and back again. "Something you two want to tell me?"

Crossing his arms across his chest, Max leans against the doorframe. "Do you want to answer that or do you want me to?" He cocks a brow at Nix, who looks as if she'd rather have God strike her down than have this conversation.

"Just . . ." She takes two steps toward me then stops. "I need to get dressed." She points at Max. "Don't say a word." Then she jogs to the back of the house where the master bedroom is.

I clear my throat. "She's gonna come out here and try to convince me that you two just get together and hang out half naked in a completely platonic way, isn't she?"

Max presses his lips together and shrugs.

"How long has this been going on?"

He lifts his palms and then points in the direction Nix disappeared as if to remind me that she told him not to say anything.

When Nix reappears, she's put on a pair of shorts. She scowls at Max. "Go get dressed," she hisses.

"You're wearing my shirt."

She flinches, and I laugh. "Nix, it's not a big deal."

A red, beaten-up Escort pulls into the drive, and a teenager with a mop of black hair climbs out with a

193

pizza box.

"*There's* the pizza," Max says.

He climbs down the porch steps to pay the driver, and Nix drags me into the house and then into her office. She shuts the door behind me, leans against it, and closes her eyes. "I *swear* it's not what it looks like."

"If by that you mean you aren't about to ease some post-sex munchies with pizza, then I think you're a big liar."

Her eyes fly open. "It just . . . happened. Please don't tell Hanna."

"Oh, sweetie." I wrap my arms around her and hug tightly, even as she keeps her body stiff as a board. "Max doesn't *belong* to Hanna. She chose Nate, remember?"

I release her, but she still hasn't relaxed.

"It just happened," she repeats. "He brought Claire in for her well-child visit and somehow I brought up that my garage door opener wasn't working and he offered to come fix it and then he fixed it and we were laughing and he kissed me and it was so nice that I kissed him back, and the next thing I know, our clothes are coming off." She takes a breath. Finally.

"Sounds great. So, it was the kind of kissing that made your clothes magically disappear, huh?"

She swallows. "Pretty much."

"My favorite kind of kissing." I smile, but despite my attempts to keep this light, Nix still looks mortified.

"It seemed harmless, but nothing's going to come of it. I promise."

"I'm still confused about where the problem is."

"He was in love with Hanna. Hanna was in love with him."

She's so cute. "And now Hanna's married to Nate and raising his babies, and you and Max are both single, healthy, consenting adults."

"You make it sound simple," she mutters. "When, in my head, it's like this complex equation."

I sigh. "Compared to *my* love life, yours is like basic addition."

"And yours is more like advanced trigonometry, huh?"

I nod and swallow. "And, Nix, I was never any good at math." Then I cry. I don't want to, but the tears spring to my eyes and roll down my cheeks and my breathing goes choppy.

She hugs me and strokes my hair.

"I'm sorry I lied to you," I blubber. "There are secrets that aren't mine to tell. But you're right. I'm giving him the chance to hurt me again. Only problem is, the alternative hurts more."

"I don't understand," she says. "How can you let him break your heart all over again?"

"With some people, love becomes your air, like the oxygen that you can't live without. You need it, and once you find it, you'll do anything to keep it."

"Sam's your air."

I nod into her shoulder.

"You don't have to tell me Sam's secrets, but I want you to know you can talk to me if you need someone."

There's a knock, then Max pokes his head into the

office. The smile falls off his face when he sees me. "Who do I need to castrate?"

"Sam," Nix says. "But only if I don't do it first."

Max walks into the office and pulls me out of Nix's arms and into his. His compassion brings the tears back full force.

"You're the best thing that ever happened to him," he whispers in my ear. "If he marries her, he's a fool."

CHAPTER
TWENTY-TWO

Sam

MY HEAD IS POUNDING, and I feel as if someone poured a vat of sawdust into my mouth while I slept. I turn to bury my face in my pillow and roll into a warm body.

Liz.

I pull her against me. Apparently, every inch of me is hungover except my dick. *It* is doing just fine.

She moans as I slip my hand inside her robe and find her breasts. They're firm and full and—

Not Liz.

I jerk away and spring upright in bed, and my head

screams in protest.

I'm in the hotel room in New York City, and I'm in bed with Sabrina Guy.

"Are you okay?" She sits up and straightens her robe. Her cheeks are flushed and her eyes bright. She doesn't seem afflicted by the same demon hangover that has taken over my head.

My stomach lurches. How in the holy-loving fuck did I end up in her bed?

"Sam?"

I rush to the bathroom and vomit, the demon in my head screaming with every movement.

Fifteen minutes later, when my stomach's empty, my teeth are brushed, and I've had a hot shower, I return to the suite. I'm sick of this game playing. I'm sick of pretending that I'm with Sabrina, and sick of having to hide my relationship with Liz. And this is only the beginning.

I want to tell the world that *Liz* is my girl now, not Sabrina.

Sabrina's sitting on the couch, her arms folded. She's pissed.

"Good morning, Mr. Bradshaw."

I spin around—more demon screaming—and see Erin McDaniel making herself a cup of coffee in the kitchenette.

She gives me a once-over and arches a brow. "Had a little too much fun last night, did you?"

"When did you get here?" I shake my head and hold up a hand. "Never mind. Don't speak. I don't care enough to listen."

"That's definitely the strongest reaction any guy's ever had to waking up in bed next to me," Sabrina says.

I close my eyes and exhale slowly. "It's not personal."

"Right. Sure. Whatever."

I feel like hell. I look at the clock and see it's after noon. "Shit. Aren't we supposed to be heading home by now?"

Sabrina pulls her mouth into a pout. "Last night, we decided we'd stay another day. Don't you remember?"

"I don't remember shit from last night, Sabrina." I have snippets. Sabrina and I, drinking in the corner of the hotel bar. We were laughing about something, and then she spotted a journalist on the other side of the bar and told me to kiss her. I remember she put her tongue in my mouth and I pushed her away. Then we ordered another round of drinks. It gets pretty sketchy after that.

What did I do? "Did we . . .?" I wave to the bed.

Sabrina shrugs. "I don't remember, but I think . . . maybe." She gives a pointed look to Erin. They're having a silent conversation.

Fuck. "I need to call Liz."

"You need to call your ex-girlfriend and explain why you're spending another day with your fiancée?" Erin asks.

"She's not my fiancée." I'm too hungover to put up with this crap.

"And *she's* not your *anything,*" Sabrina says.

I just stare at her. She seems different this morning. Self-satisfied. The phrase *cat that ate the canary* comes to mind.

"Why now, Sam?" Sabrina asks. "You two could have been together all this time, but you wait until it fucks with my life and *my* reputation to fuck around again."

"We're not fucking around."

"So you're serious about her? That thing with your dad doesn't bother you anymore?"

I go cold. "I'm not talking about that with you."

"I just think it's sad."

"It doesn't matter what you think. It's not your business, Sabrina."

"Funny. Neither is that tape." She lifts her arms. "But here I am."

"Stop it," Erin says. "Both of you. You're like children."

"Then let's back off." I look to Erin. She's the puppet master in all of this. "We've given them their quotes and their clips of us together. Let's stop while we're ahead."

"Stop?" Sabrina pushes off the couch and stalks toward me. Funny. She doesn't look all that hungover. "You think they won't notice if we just ignore each other for the rest of the campaign? And I don't know about you, but I don't see any condom wrappers around here anywhere. What if I'm pregnant from last night, huh?"

My stomach heaves again. "This has gotten out of control."

"You made me a promise, Sam," Erin says. "All I ask is that you follow through and don't fuck us over."

"Especially for a woman you have no future with

anyway," Sabrina adds.

"I don't want to hear your opinion about my future with Liz," I growl at Sabrina. "After Tuesday's primaries, I'm ready to tell the press we have irreconcilable differences. I don't want to do this anymore. I *can't* do this anymore and I won't."

She studies me for a beat, her eyes calculating. "Great. We'll just make one phone call and get those transcripts of her conversations with your father leaked to the press." She turns to Erin. "That shouldn't be a problem, should it?"

"One phone call," Erin says. "Shall I do it now or later?"

"You wouldn't—"

"Oh, yes we would," Sabrina says. "Try it."

These two are more dangerous than they look, and I feel like the fool who suddenly realizes he's been consorting with the devil. "You were never going to get me visitations with Lilly, were you? Was the DNA test even real?"

"Oh, it was real," Sabrina says. "I made it my business to know if she was really yours long before you even knew she was born."

"Why do you care so much?" I ask.

"Because I've sacrificed everything," she says, her eyes blazing and looking a little wild. "*Everything.* Do you get that? The only thing I have left to lose is you, and I won't let that happen."

CHAPTER
TWENTY-THREE

Liz

I STAYED AT NIX'S last night, shamefully ending any additional sexy times she doubtlessly had planned with Max. I let her comfort me in every way she could without me telling her what I couldn't, and after that I was too emotionally exhausted to drive home.

When I do get home, there's a sexy man leaning against my door with a couple of Starbucks cups and a magazine.

"Hi, George." Too bad it's not the sexy man I want to see.

He hands me the cup. "I wasn't sure what you liked

from Starbucks, but I figured anything with lots of sugar would do, and I got you a double mocha. I'm guessing you could use it."

I probably look as wrung out as I feel. "I'm okay."

"You two fought."

I shake my head. "I don't know what you're talking about."

"These walls aren't that thick, Liz, and I was home last night."

Unsure how to respond, I take a long drink—*heaven*. "Come on in," I say, opening the door.

I'm not in the mood for company, but if George is going to do sweet things like bring me sugar-laden coffee on a Saturday morning, it's time we have a talk.

The couch seems too intimate after Sam told me he caught George looking down my shirt, so I lead the way to the table and take a seat.

He takes the seat across from me and puts the magazine facedown in front of him.

"What is that?" I ask.

"*Stars Like Us*, this morning's edition."

I frown. "The gossip rag?" That's the magazine that first got its hands on the sex tape.

"My employer."

I draw in a sharp breath. I knew he worked for a magazine, but I never asked which and I never thought . . . "No."

He holds up a hand. "I have no intentions of telling anyone at work about my neighbor's evening activities. That's not exactly my job anyway. I work the tech side of things."

"There's nothing between me and Sam." And I am so sick of lying that I'm determined to make it true. At least until he doesn't have to pretend to be with Sabrina anymore.

"Good to know," George says. He flips the magazine over and nudges it across the table.

My heart rises into my throat, bringing a couple of gallons of stomach acid with it. It hurts to look at the couple on the cover. "I don't understand."

"I guess the bride- and groom-to-be got a little frisky after picking out rings yesterday. One of our New York photographers got a tip that they'd be in the hotel bar last night, and when he showed up, they put on quite a show."

The cover shows Sam and Sabrina in a corner booth of a swanky bar. She's straddling his lap, her skirt hitched high on her hips, and his hands are in her wild red hair as she kisses him.

"I'm not trying to hurt you, Liz," George says. "I feel like you need a friend right now."

Why would this hurt me? That's what I should say, but the words won't come. I open up the magazine and find the article, "America's Sweethearts Still Hot for Each Other." The two-page spread isn't so much an article as it is a collage of pictures taken of the two of them in the bar last night.

I'm going to throw up.

I don't know how long I stare at the pictures, but they've gone blurry behind my tears when George pulls the magazine away.

"I'm sorry. He's a rat bastard, Liz."

Rat bastard. Isn't that supposed to be his father, not him? "He's a good guy. He just—"

"Do you even see yourself?" George asks. "Have you looked in the mirror in the last five months and faced the sadness in your eyes? Because I've seen it every day. I don't know what they think they're doing behind the scenes of that campaign, but I hate what this is doing to you. Don't let him hurt you anymore. You deserve *so much* better."

I take a deep breath and wipe my eyes. George works for *Stars Like Us.* I need to make sure I don't give anything away he could use against the campaign. My gut tells me I can trust him, but my gut's useless. "His engagement doesn't have anything to do with the campaign."

George grunts. "I suppose the next thing you're going to tell me is that the video is recent?" He holds up a hand. "Relax. I can't prove anything. I just have my suspicions."

"What do you mean?" I take a long drink of my coffee. I'm counting on the sugar to pick me up and help me keep my poker face, but it might be a lost cause.

"Do you ever wonder who leaked that sex tape? I mean, normal people keep that kind of thing under lock and key, but someone in a political family would be especially judicious about their privacy."

And Christine even more so than Sabrina. "I don't know," I say. "I guess I never really thought about it." But it's a good question. A really good question. "Didn't they say Sabrina's computer was hacked?" But why would Sabrina have her mom's sex tape on her computer? That doesn't make sense. Was that a lie too?

"So, one of our journalists has this source—I don't know who it was, of course. That's top-secret stuff. But he brought me that recording the day it aired and he had me look into it. He wanted to make sure it was legit, because it seemed like too good of a scoop to be true. I was able to tell him when it was recorded."

I straighten. "You were?"

"Yeah. Digital videos have information embedded in them, and I could see it was created only a couple of days before his source handed it over. But then I met Sam in person, and I started to get suspicious. He looks older now than he does in the video. His physique is even different. I suspect someone created a new file—tailored an old video of Sam and the governor to leak to the media so it would look like Sam and Sabrina were having an affair. Her hair used to be longer, didn't it?"

"That's a pretty hefty accusation."

He holds out his palms. "Not an accusation, a suspicion. And one that dies with me. You have my word. I'm only bringing it up now because I want you to know the kind of people you're involved with. The question is, who would go to the trouble to alter the video and leak it to the press? Presumably Roe's campaign might benefit from the leak, but why change it when—if I'm correct—the original date stamp would have destroyed Guy's campaign?"

"That's another good question," I say softly. But I think I already know the answer.

My phone buzzes with a text alert, and I pull it from

my purse.

Sam: *Don't look at the magazines. I can explain.*

But I can't think of any explanation that will work for me. I've known I was playing with fire, and it's more obvious than ever that I need to break it off with Sam.

"These people aren't messing around, Liz, and if I know there's more between you and Bradshaw than meets the eye, then I guarantee someone else does too. Just be careful. Please?"

"I will."

He stands to go.

"George," I call when he reaches the door.

"Yeah?"

I stare at the image of the man I love groping Sabrina's ass. There's going to be a big party at headquarters on Tuesday night as the numbers come in from South Dakota. And though Christine will be at her headquarters there, Sabrina will be here in Indianapolis. And she'll probably have Sam by her side. My first instinct is to ask George to go with me, but after everything he's done for me, that seems cruel. "I can't offer you anything other than friendship right now, but I want you to know I appreciate you. You've been good to me."

He smiles, a lovely, charming smile. "Any time."

SOMETHING REAL

* * *

Sam

"You two make the most *adorable* couple," a white-haired woman tells Sabrina and me. "You know, back in my youth, my husband and I liked to explore a little, too." She lowers her voice. "*Sexually* speaking."

Dear God. If I have to hear one more person tell me about their sex life, I'm going to fucking lose it. I don't know what it is about having a sex tape leaked that makes people think you want details of their private lives.

"We thank you for your support," Sabrina says. "It's been a rough couple of weeks."

I spot Liz by Christine's office and do a double take. I can never be sure it's her. In the two days since I got back from New York, I've seen her on a daily basis. I spotted her at the gas station, at the gym, standing in line at the bank. Of course, it was never her. The real Liz wasn't any of those places. She was somewhere working very hard to dodge my calls and avoid my visits. The only word I've had from her since we hung up on Friday night was a Saturday-morning text of *I can't do this.*

I couldn't handle not talking to her any longer, so I came to headquarters to find her, but the place is packed with staffers and volunteers all running on the high of Christine's spike in the polls.

If Liz would just let me explain those pictures . . . not that I remember enough to explain.

"Would you ladies excuse me for a moment?"

"Of course," Sabrina says. "I'll be in my office. Make sure you come give me a kiss before you leave."

I give a noncommittal smile and make my way across the room, doing my best to smile politely to everyone who greets me. Truth is, I feel like a predator. The only thing I care about is getting to Liz. The only thing I care about is having her in my arms again. I won't be able to sleep until I prove to myself I didn't lose her by getting trashed and falling into bed with Sabrina.

"You're a hard woman to track down," I say when I see her.

Liz turns around, eyes wide when she spots me. She ducks her head. "Excuse me."

I step into her path before she can get away. I lower my head so only she can hear me. "Meet me in the conference room in five minutes."

She flinches. "I'm working."

"Meet me anyway."

Her jaw tightens, and she looks left then right to make sure no one heard what I said. "Fine."

She's pissed. No problem. If there's anything I'm good at, it's changing her state of mind.

I wait, watching until Liz says something to one of the other staffers and heads to the conference room. Thirty seconds later, I follow her.

When I enter the room, her back's to me, her fingers grazing a stack of magazines on the table. As soon as I lock the door behind me, she spins, her hands on her hips.

"I'm done," she says. "This is the last time you get me alone."

I take a step back, and my body hits the door. "Done?"

"You thought you'd bring me in here, throw my skirt over my head, and fuck me? To be fair, I guess that's what's been happening lately, but I'm done."

"What are you talking about?"

"It's just sex, right? Hell, maybe I should bill you. What's the going rate for a screw these days? And do I get more for the times you tied me up?"

"I *never* said it was just sex."

"But that *is* all it is, Sam. You're planning your wedding to another woman and visiting me for your booty calls. I let you fuck me at work when your pretend fiancée was in the room next door, for God's sake."

"You're talking crazy." Something in my stomach warns me that she's not. It's that hitching feeling you get at the top of the first hill on a roller coaster, right before the bottom falls out. Except there's no thrill in this. Only terror.

"There's one way we can be together." She drops her gaze to the floor, like she can't stomach looking at me. "You can walk out there and tell everyone that your engagement is no more. Admit it was a sham, or say you two struggled under the media scrutiny. You can tell the world you're not with her, and *then* I can be with you. She's poison."

"I know she is." I swallow the lump in my throat. "But I can't." This isn't just about me getting to meet my child anymore. I can't subject Liz to the humiliation that would follow Sabrina releasing her conversations with my father. "Too many people would get hurt." You *would get hurt.*

"Then I can't be with you."

I never expected an ultimatum. Not from Liz. "You don't understand."

"Maybe I understand too well." She grabs a magazine from the stack and presents it to me. As if I haven't seen those horrible pictures for myself.

"Is this about those tabloid pictures? I've wanted to talk to you, but you avoided my calls. We were in the bar, and a photographer showed up. We were acting for the cameras."

"You're one hell of an actor."

"Liz, listen."

"I'll listen when you're not with her anymore. When you're living *truth* instead of a lie. Not until then."

"You want *truth*? I don't even remember it. I don't remember her climbing into my lap, and I certainly don't remember falling into fucking bed with her." There it is. The summit, the moment everything falls out from under you. I intended to tell her, but not like this. Never like this.

Her face creases with hurt and she curls into herself. "You slept with her?"

"I—" It's my turn to look away. Just the memory of waking up next to Sabrina is enough to make my stomach churn. "I don't know, but I can't lie to you. We woke up in bed together, and both of us drank too much the night before to remember what happened. I'd remember *something* if I slept with her, wouldn't I?"

But I can see on her face that it doesn't matter. She's too hurt by the possibility.

"I don't even *like* her. I don't remember what happened. You were pissed at me and I drank too much. Don't walk away from me. I can't lose you again. I don't care about all the bullshit behind us, Liz. All I care about is tomorrow and the tomorrow after that. All that matters is knowing I get to have them all with you."

She closes her eyes. She's so beautiful, her lashes resting against her cheeks. I want to memorize her. Even like this, even angry with me, and hurt. I want to take her in until she becomes part of me.

She swallows and takes a deep breath. "While we're talking about the truth, you should know I'm the one who told Connor about Asia. I didn't know she was pregnant and I didn't know what he was going to do, but after I saw you with her, I'm the one who gave him her name. And I'm sorry about that. You have no idea how sorry. But you need to know that I played a part."

My breath leaves me in a rush. "What?" I'm surrounded by people I can't trust. The idea that Liz had something to do with the baby being taken away from me is too much.

I'm so afraid she's right. This is over. And we've been fooling ourselves.

"You hurt me, Sam, but I have to take some blame too. You and I both knew this wasn't going to end in happily ever after," she whispers. Pain is all over her face and her eyes fill with tears. "How could it?"

CHAPTER
TWENTY-FOUR

Liz

Sam: *I forgive you for telling Connor. Please don't give up on us.*

"PLEASE STOP CRYING," Nix says. "Please, please, please, Liz. I can handle tears but I suck with emotional breakdowns."

"I'm sorry," George says. "She's been like this since she got home from work. She told me to drive her here." He hands her my phone. "She'd just gotten this text."

Nix reads the text and frowns then looks at me. She

takes my shoulders in her hands and dips her head until I meet her eyes. "Stop crying long enough to tell me *one thing* I can do to help you. Just one thing, big or small."

"Call Hanna."

When my twin arrives, she takes one look at me and wraps me in her arms. "It's okay," she whispers, stroking my hair. "We're going to figure this out. I promise. Just breathe."

Sam

My father steps into his office, and his jaw drops when he spots me. "Sam?"

I haven't spoken a single unnecessary word to my father in more than five months. Maybe he doesn't deserve any better than that, but somehow losing Liz has changed the way I see my relationship with my father. I've been punishing myself as much as I've been punishing him.

It's not just because of what he did with Liz—though that alone makes me want to punch him all over again. It's what happened with Asia.

After the shock from Liz's confession wore off, I realized her guilt was misplaced. Maybe she gave Connor Asia's name, but that doesn't make her responsible for the blackmail. And now more than ever,

I need to confront the man who was.

There was no reason for Connor to blackmail her into lying to me. No reason but my father. So for five months, I've been carrying around the special resentment of a man who's had something precious stolen from him by someone he thought he could trust.

"Can we talk?" I ask.

He nods and shuts the door. "What can I do for you?" His voice cracks on the last word, and he clears his throat to cover it. "I'm glad you're here."

I drop my gaze to my hands. Fuck. This is just as hard as I thought it would be. "I think we need to be straight with each other."

"Okay." Instead of sitting behind his desk, he takes the chair next to mine. "About the wedding? If you need anything, just say the word. Money, special favors . . . whatever we can do. I want the best for you and Sabrina."

Me and Sabrina. Oh, hell. He's not the only liar in this family. I've been doing him proud. "It's not about the wedding. It's about Asia."

He frowns. "Asia?"

"The stripper I knocked up? She came around last winter asking for hush money."

He inclines his chin. "Right. I remember. Is she giving you trouble again?"

"I found the baby," I say, looking him in the eye. "I did some digging and hired a private investigator, and I found the baby. The one you blackmailed her into telling me she aborted."

"Wait. Slow down. What?"

"Don't you dare punish her for this. You're the one who—"

"I didn't blackmail anyone, Sam. When you came to me before Christmas, I had Connor offer her money to stay quiet about the abortion—but you knew about that. I didn't even know about the baby before then."

"Why should I believe you?"

"What would I gain by lying to you?"

I wrap my hands around the arms of the chair and squeeze as I grit my teeth. "I don't trust you."

"Right." He exhales heavily. "I earned that, I guess. But Sam? What do I have to lose? It's not like you can hate me more than you already do. I'm beginning to believe you'll never forgive me for what happened with Liz."

Even hearing him speak her name make me sick. I don't want my father anywhere near Liz, not even in his thoughts.

"I'm telling you the truth, Sam. I didn't have anything to do with Asia."

"Then why did Connor give her money to make her lie to me?"

He frowns. "Connor?"

"He works for you, Dad. I know he was looking into me and trying clean up my 'messes' for your campaign."

"But you're talking about something that happened over two years ago. He was only working for me part time back then. I swear I wasn't behind it."

Something prickles at the back of my neck. I think he's telling the truth. So who would do that to me? I can only think of one person.

"I made it my business to know if she was really yours long before you even knew she was born."

"Big night tomorrow at Guy headquarters," Dad says. "I assume you're going."

"Yeah. I'll be there."

"Your mom and I are glad to see you and Sabrina together. That's all we wanted, you know, was for you to be happy. And . . ." He clears his throat. "I apologize that I got in the way of that with Liz."

I look down at my hands. The apology feels better than I would have imagined, and maybe I would have had it months ago if I had been willing to talk to him. "I'm not *happy* with Sabrina."

"What? Why not? Can we help?"

"I'm not *with* Sabrina, Dad. The sex tape was old— from when I was seventeen and having an affair with Sabrina's mother."

"Then why—" The confusion falls off his face as what I'm saying registers. "You and . . . Christine?"

I nod.

"Christ." He looks at the ceiling—inhales, exhales. "Don't tell your mother. She'd tear the woman apart."

"It was consensual."

"You were seventeen."

I shrug.

"So you and Sabrina? That's just a cover-up?"

"Initially, I agreed to pretend it was Sabrina because I knew that tape would be the end of Christine's campaign, but then one lie spiraled into another, and now I'm being blackmailed into continuing to plan a wedding I never intend to have."

His jaw tightens. "Who's blackmailing you?"

"Sabrina and Christine's campaign manager. Somehow they got transcripts of the conversations you and Liz had on Something Real and they're threatening to release them if I don't continue to play along."

"The fuck they will." He reaches for his phone.

"Dad, stop," I say when he brings it to his ear. "That wouldn't just hurt me and Liz, it would destroy your campaign."

He flinches. "But don't I deserve that?"

"Dad—"

He settles the phone in its cradle. "Your mother wants to leave me. I know she's only staying for you kids and the campaign. But some days I feel like if I were still managing the bank instead of pursuing a career in politics, she'd be gone. She'd be happier. She's only staying to protect my chance to win this race."

It's my turn to flinch. "I'm sorry."

"Don't apologize. I deserve it. She should have left me years ago. Hell, she probably shouldn't have married me to begin with."

"So let her go, Dad. If you want her to be happy, tell her to do the thing that will bring her happiness. Consequences be damned."

"I—" He drags a hand through his hair. "I thought I was the one who was supposed to be giving you advice."

I give a humorless laugh. "Go for it. What can I do about Sabrina? Every day I pretend to be with her, it hurts Liz, and I'm done hurting her. I want to be with her."

He exhales slowly. "You really love her."

I nod.

"Jesus, I'm a bastard."

"I've been telling myself that about you for months, and take it from me, it doesn't actually make anything better."

"You want my advice?"

"Yeah. I'd do anything to get her back."

Leaning back in his chair, he crosses his arms and gives me a cocky smile. "Tell her the truth about everything and tell her to do the thing that will bring her the most happiness. Consequences be damned."

I grunt and stand. "That's pretty good advice."

"Don't worry about my campaign. I'm sick to death of seeing my family suffer for my mistakes. If the truth comes out, I'll handle it then."

"Thank you," I whisper. When I get to the door, I stop and turn to my dad. "If Connor was only working part time for you then, where else was he working?"

"He had an internship in Indianapolis at the governor's office. But from what I understand, he mostly did work for Sabrina."

CHAPTER
TWENTY-FIVE

Liz

"I WANT TO MAKE A TOAST," Hanna says. "To the best friends a girl can have."

"Hear, hear!" Maggie says, hoisting her beer.

Because we're in New Hope and my friends are who they are, we ended up at Brady's.

Nix swore me to secrecy about her and Max, of course, but judging by the way Max is looking at her tonight, it won't be a secret for long.

It's good to be here surrounded by friends, rather than stuck in my little apartment dwelling on the mistakes I've made and whether or not I made the right decision in giving Sam an ultimatum.

I spot Della seated at the bar. "Excuse me, you guys," I say. "I need to take care of something." I leave my beer behind—I've barely touched it anyway—and take the seat next to Sam's sister. "How are you?"

She turns and jerks in surprise when she sees it's me. "Oh. Um. I'm good. Okay. Fine." Her shoulders slouch. "Life's a bitch."

I bite my lip. "Want to talk about it?"

Her eyes fill with tears. "I don't want my brother to marry Sabrina," she says, surprising me. I assumed her tears were about Connor. She shakes her head. "She's not good people."

I draw in a breath, but my chest feels tight with the secret that's not mine to tell. "I thought you liked her."

She shakes her head. "I was stupid to ever think she was my friend. She just used me to control Connor."

"Where is Connor tonight? Are you two okay?"

She shrugs. "I don't know where he is. I think we're over."

I drop my gaze to the bar and trace a crack in the wood. "Della, I think I owe you an apology. Last summer when I went home with Connor . . . it was a mistake. I thought you'd broken up with him, but even if you had I never should have—"

"It's not your fault." She stirs her red drink with her straw. "Sabrina told me he was sleeping with you, so I packed my bags and left. I can't blame him for being fed up with me at that point."

"Sabrina told you that?"

She nods. "Yeah. He works for her sometimes and I

thought maybe she knew something I didn't."

"I wasn't." I reach over and put my hand on her wrist. "I screwed up, but I never would have messed with him while you two were together."

"Yeah, I know that now."

"Why would Sabrina say that?"

Her lips turn up in a humorless smile. "Because Sam was on a crusade to win your heart, and Sabrina wouldn't have it."

Sabrina was the redhead in the bar that night. Holy shit. "She told Connor to take me home?"

"No, she's never that obvious. But he confessed later that right after I blew up and left, she called and said she'd stopped by town and noticed you were at Brady's, looking like you needed a friend." She lifts her eyes to mine, and the normal Della bitchiness is gone. Instead, she just looks sad. "That's all she had to do. Connor's always had a soft spot for you."

"Jesus." A shiver ricochets from the base of my spine and up to my neck. "That's conniving."

"See why I don't trust her?" She shakes her head. "Connor and I? We were played. Sabrina's a fucking genius when it comes to playing people. But Sam was always above it somehow. That's why I can't figure out this engagement."

My stomach churns when I think about him being in that hotel room with her. He's made his own decisions when it comes to Sabrina and the tape, but what if he's being played? What if he truly can't remember that night with her because someone doesn't want him to remember? What if George is right, and someone in the campaign tampered with it to make it look recent? And what if that person was Sabrina?

* * *

I'm locking my apartment the next morning when I see Connor standing in the hall. "What are you doing here?"

"Can we talk?"

He shrugs. "Della kicked me out and Mr. Bradshaw fired me. Not sure where else I should be."

"I don't know, Connor, but the answer isn't with me."

"I don't mean it like that." He runs a hand through his hair and sighs. "I want to do something right for once."

"I don't know what you mean by that, but I need to get to work."

"I wouldn't believe everything you see in the gossip magazines."

My stomach hitches at the reminder of the pictures of Sam and Sabrina. "I don't know what you're talking about."

"Sure you do. You're in love with Sam," Connor says. "And Sabrina did exactly what she had to do to take him away from you. She ruins lives. It's her specialty."

"*Sabrina* ruins lives? What about you? You betrayed Sam. You took his child from him."

He grimaces. "I was doing Sabrina's bidding, but I know that doesn't make it right. That's something I have to live with."

"And that's why you took me home last summer too, isn't it? I never put two and two together, but I remember a redhead at Brady's that night. That was her, wasn't it? She wanted to make sure you got me to go home with you."

"It wasn't a hardship, Liz. I didn't know Della was pregnant and Sabrina knew I was in love with you and—"

"In love with me? That's not *love*, Connor. That's sick. Seducing someone to manipulate someone else is disgusting and low."

"Sabrina was blackmailing me," he says. His face is bleak, defeated. "Still is, which is why I've been spying on Sam, but Della kicked me out and I figure I don't have anything left to lose so I'm done letting her control me."

I fold my arms. "How is she blackmailing you?"

"I'm not a good person. I did shitty things that no one was ever supposed to find out about, and she dug them up and used them to get me to do more shitty things." He gives a sad smile. "You know what's crazy? She was so damn good at convincing me I was doing something good. With Asia, she convinced me I was protecting Sam. And when she called that night last summer to let me know that you were at the bar and upset, Della had just left and I thought, 'Hey, funny how things work out.' It wasn't until months later that I learned she was the *reason* Della left that night. But this time with the tape and Sam . . . she's transparent to me now."

"What is she after?" I ask.

"All she wants is Sam. That's all she's ever wanted, and for once I want to be on the other side of things. I can't stand being part of that evil bitch's plotting anymore."

My mind is spinning. This is too much to take in at once. "Slow down. You admit you were the one who made Asia lie to Sam about the baby? His dad wasn't behind it?"

"I'm not a good person," he repeats. "But I wanted to believe she wasn't just manipulating me—that I wasn't just her puppet. But then I watched Sam get pulled into her snare and I knew you'd end up hurt. I can't fix what I've done, but I can tell you that Sam has loved you for years, and I don't believe for a second he would risk a chance to have you back in his life for a night in her bed."

"It doesn't matter," I whisper, giving up the pretense that I don't know the engagement is a sham. "I won't be his dirty secret anymore."

"Be careful," he says, picking up a suitcase I didn't notice before.

"Where are you going?"

"Back home. It's time I face my past."

CHAPTER
TWENTY-SIX

Liz

MY PHONE BUZZES in my purse and I pull it out to see another missed call from Sam. I send it to voicemail and close my eyes, trying to remember how to breathe. I gave him an ultimatum, and no matter how much I miss him, I need to stand by it.

Everyone is supposed to clear out of headquarters by four p.m. today so the party planners and the tech and light crew can set up for tonight, but I was so busy working on paperwork, I totally lost track of time.

My phone buzzes again. This time with a text.

SOMETHING REAL

Sam: *I need to talk to you before tonight.*

It hurts to ignore the message, but I make myself. He knows what he has to do if he wants to make this work. I stack my papers and shut down the computer. It's four fifteen, and the place is eerily quiet. It's never quiet. I grab my purse and head for the door.

"We were supposed to *get married*," someone says from Erin McDaniel's office.

It's Sabrina. I recognize that voice, even though right now she sounds less like a political shark and more like a petulant child.

"You were never getting married," Erin says.

"It's been the plan since I was a child. He's mine."

"That was a fantasy you concocted in your pretty little head," Erin says. "And I'm beyond sick of catering to it."

"Who asked you to cater to anything?" Sabrina says. I peek through the crack in the door and can see one side of Sabrina's face. She looks pissed. Like, scary, she-devil pissed. "You want me to let the press in on the truth about that video?"

"I'm done letting you manipulate me with that threat, Sabrina. You got what you wanted. We leaked the tape, cut the footage of your mother's face, and made it look like it was you. If you tell the world that now, I'll let them know where it came from to begin with. *You're* the one who will look like the fool. And God help you if your mother found out."

"It will still destroy her." Her voice shakes.

"I'm not convinced there's any path but destruction

for anyone tied to you."

Sabrina sighs heavily. "I won't say anything about the video. Don't worry. I have other plans."

"Please don't tell me. Plausible deniability and all that."

"If it weren't for Liz, I know this would have worked. He's addicted to her. It's ridiculous. What does she have that I don't?"

"A soul?" Erin says, but instead of snapping, Sabrina just laughs. "Whatever your plan is, understand that you can't win the heart of a man who hates you."

"He doesn't *hate* me. He has no idea what I've done."

"Soon enough, he'll find out you were behind paying Asia off. He'll find out that Connor was working as *your* little errand boy. You think he's going to want to marry you then?"

Sabrina slams her hands onto her desk. "What was I supposed to do? Let her move in with him and raise the baby like a happy little family? He's supposed to be mine. And he'd be lucky to have me."

"You think so? You, the woman who slipped him a roofie in New York? You *drugged* him, and you're lucky the press couldn't tell. I'm just glad I showed up when I did. I shudder to think what you had planned for when you got him back to your room. They call that *rape*, Sabrina, and I never thought of you as a rapist."

I throw my hand over my mouth to cover my gasp. That's why Sam can't remember.

"I am *not*. You saw him that night. He was all over me until you got there and pulled us apart."

"You drugged him."

"He was *mine*," she growls.

"Well, I think you've screwed the pooch on that one," Erin says.

"You underestimate me. I always win."

Sam

"There you are!"

The bartender hands me my beer, and I take a long pull as I turn to the person tugging on my sleeve.

I nearly cough the liquid up when I see that it's Liz. "I've been looking for you," I say quietly. I scan the crowd quickly, looking for Sabrina, who'd flip to see me talking to Liz. It seems like everyone is here tonight—my father, Della, Connor, and all of Guy's volunteers and staffers. Sabrina thinks I'm here for her, but the truth is I'm done letting her hold my balls in a vise. It ends tonight.

"We need to talk," Liz says.

"Yes." It's hard to speak. I just want to hold her. God, everything is so fucked up. "I'm going to do it tonight."

"Do what?" Her brow creases in confusion.

"I'm going to tell everyone that Sabrina and I aren't getting married," I say softly. "Because I'm in love with someone else."

Her lips part and she squeezes her eyes shut. "Shit. You can't do that. She's too dangerous."

"I know. She threatened to leak the transcripts of you and Riverrat to the press. I've been trying to protect you, but I think I've figured out a way to protect you from that and still get away from the charade."

She squeezes my wrist. "She drugged you, Sam. That's why you can't remember that night. I overheard her talking with Erin, and Erin said Sabrina slipped you a roofie. She's crazy. Promise me you'll be careful."

"Liz!" A girl with spiky black hair grabs her arm and tugs her toward the stage. "We have to get the slideshow ready."

"Be careful!" Liz says.

I nod. She could ask me to lie across a path of hot coals so she could cross, and I'd do it. Anything to have her talking to me again. Anything to see that hurt wiped from her eyes.

The numbers are rolling in and looking good for Christine. There's little doubt now that she'll have a spot on the presidential ballot in November. I won't let Sabrina manipulate me for another six months. I don't know why I didn't think of turning her tricks back on her sooner.

Suddenly, the room erupts with cheers, and I turn toward the big TVs behind the stage to see what's going on.

"Roe is giving his concession speech!" someone squeals next to me. "Guy won the primaries!"

The cheers die down as Sabrina takes the stage, mic in hand. Christine's at the satellite HQ in South Dakota, so Sabrina will give the speeches to this group tonight. "This is all because of you!" she calls into the mic, and the crowd roars. "Can I have my handsome fiancé join me on the stage, please?"

Everyone turns as the spotlight scans the crowd and eventually lands on me. I force a smile and head to the stage.

CHAPTER TWENTY-SEVEN

Liz

SAM CLIMBS ONTO THE STAGE, and I want to stop him. That feeling is niggling my gut again—my stupid, untrustworthy gut. I don't want him near her. But it's not just that. Something tells me he shouldn't be on the stage, and I edge closer to the front as he whispers something in Sabrina's ear.

Her happy mask falls for three beats of my heart, but then she recovers herself and plants a hard kiss on his lips.

He's standing so stiff that I can't believe anyone in the audience is buying it when he slings his arms around her shoulders.

"Where are you going?" Grace asks.

I'm at the front of the crowd now. I could reach out and touch Sam if I wanted to. And God, I want to. My gut screams at me to get him off that stage.

"What are you doing?" Grace says, grabbing my arm. "You're worrying me."

Sabrina snuggles into Sam's embrace and grins at the crowd. "We're the luckiest people in the world, and I'm not just talking about Sam and me. I'm talking about all of us. Everyone in this room is blessed to be able to vote for my mom in November!"

The crowd cheers, and Sabrina sweeps the floor in front of her with her foot.

I see the switch taped to the stage the second her foot connects with it, and I grab Sam's hand and tug. "Sam!"

Everything seems to happen at once. Something explodes in the scaffolding holding the lights above the stage, and I dive for the floor, my grip tight on Sam's hand. His eyes go wide as he sees the explosion, and he follows me to the floor. His big body covers mine and the lights come down with a crash. The room erupts into the chaotic symphony of equipment crashing to the stage, lights breaking, and the hissing and popping of electrical fires.

When everything but the panicked crowd quiets, Sam lifts up on his forearms and brushes my hair from my face. "Are you okay?" he asks quietly.

I nod, but when I catch sight of the stage behind him, I gasp. Sabrina's body is limp and pinned under the lighting equipment.

"You saved me," Sam says. "How did you know?"

"I had a gut feeling."

Sirens roar outside of headquarters, and moments later, Sam and I are separated as the emergency personnel gets to work.

* * *

Sam

Sabrina is alive. Not well, and not happy, but alive.

She's in bed in a blue hospital gown, the burns on her face and neck bandaged, her broken legs in casts. If it hadn't been for Liz, she'd have been even worse, if not dead, but when Liz pulled me off the stage, I had my arm around Sabrina and she moved several feet forward from the bulk of the crashing lights and equipment.

"Why?" I ask. It's the first time we've talked since I whispered in her ear on the stage letting her know that we'd reverse-engineered the code on the Something Real site to make it look like the conversations between Riverrat69 and Tink24 were between her and Connor, not Liz and my dad. It was Connor's idea, and my little brother is just brainy enough to make it work. "Why did you try to kill me?"

"You were supposed to be mine." Her face crumples pathetically behind the bandages. "Our parents talked about it since we were kids. 'Sam and Sabrina,' they'd say, 'even their names sound perfect together.' They set me up for heartbreak by dangling you in front of my face. My mother knew I was in love with you and—"

"You couldn't have been in love with me, Sabrina. We hardly knew each other."

"Maybe *you* hardly knew *me*, but I knew you. I loved you. And she seduced you just because she could. She took you away from me."

"I was never yours," I whisper.

"You were mine, and since you couldn't see it, ending it tonight was the only way we could be together."

Ryann cracks the door and gives me a tentative smile. "Are you ready?"

It's time. There's a buzz of voices outside, and when I crack the blinds to look, I see the parking lot is littered with reporters and news vans.

"Yeah, I'll meet you in the hall." When I turn back to Ryann, her face is stark white. "Everything is going to be okay, Ry. I promise."

She leaves, and I look at Sabrina one last time. "Goodbye, Sabrina. I hope I never see you again."

When I exit the room, Christine Guy is waiting for me. "Are you sure you don't want to go in there?" I ask her.

"I don't want to look at my daughter right now," Christine says with a shaky smile. "I'm just so sorry." She folds her arms in front of her. "You know, about everything. I've definitely made mistakes." She cuts her eyes to Sabrina's door. "A lot more than I realized, apparently."

"You ready for this?" her lawyer asks.

I nod and pull on my suit jacket. "As ready as I'll ever be." I wave to the police officer guarding Sabrina's door. "Thank you."

The lawyer stays by our side as we make our way to the front of the hospital and out to the awaiting press.

The second I step out the doors, the questions come rapid fire.

"Do you have a comment in response to the allegations that Sabrina Guy sabotaged the lighting at headquarters and was intending to have you killed?"

"Have you read the suicide note she left in her office?"

"Was the stress of the campaign just too much for her?"

Christine stops at one outstretched microphone, and everyone silences. "Right now, we are focusing on getting Sabrina the best medical and psychiatric care available."

"Who was the woman who pulled you off the stage?" another reporter asks me, shoving a microphone in my face. "How did she know?"

"She was an old friend who also works for the Guy campaign," I say. "She saw Sabrina reach for the switch with her foot and she knew something wasn't right. I'm grateful for her fast thinking."

"That will be all," the lawyer says, holding out his hand as we make it to the car.

"Where to now?" Christine asks.

"I need to go home," I say. "I need to see a man

about a dog."

* * *

I open the door and squeak when a dog comes running toward me. For a second, I think maybe I went into the wrong house, but it's Princess, and this is definitely my place.

"What are you doing here, girl?" I sink to my haunches to scratch her head, and she licks my face. "Did you know I needed these kisses today, huh?"

"I might have told her."

I look up to see Sam walking out of the kitchen, a glass of wine in each hand. "Did she need a home? Were they going to put her down?"

Princess whines and licks me again.

Sam settles the wine glasses on the mantel and squats next to the dog and me. "She did need a home, and Ryann said she missed you while you were gone. It made me realize Riverrat was all wrong about one thing."

My lips part, and my eyes sting. "What's that?"

"He said you didn't need a dog. He said you needed a man, instead." He takes a deep breath and exhales slowly. "He also said a bunch of other stuff I'd prefer to scour from my brain, but my point is, he was wrong. You need a dog. You need *this* dog. Because you're so full of love and goodness, it just spills out of you. Princess could use some of that. But you don't need a man."

I blink at him. "I don't?"

"No, Rowdy, you're just fine on your own. You don't need me or George or Connor. You don't even need those girls of yours, who I suspect would cut off the dick of any guy who tried to hurt you." He skims his fingertips over my cheek, his Adam's apple bobbing as he swallows. "I don't need you to need me, but I'm hoping you can forgive me for being an idiot. And I'm hoping you *want* me. Because I heard on the news my wedding's been called off."

"It has?" I squeak.

"Yeah, turns out my fiancée was a crazy bitch, and she's being brought up on charges of my attempted murder. I'm sure you can understand how that caused a rift between us."

I laugh despite myself and wipe my palms against my wet cheeks.

"So if you want me, if you'll *have* me, I swear to you I will fight for us with every breath."

"I do." My cheeks are wet again and my vision's blurry. "I want you very much."

"Thank God," he murmurs. Then he lowers his mouth to mine and kisses me the way a man should kiss a woman when they're starting their happily-ever-after.

EPILOGUE

Sam

"Could I pull you away from that computer for dinner?"

"What?" Liz looks up from her laptop and blinks at me. She's cute when she gets in the zone like that. It's as if she forgets where she is.

"Dinner," I repeat. "Food, wine, maybe even some sex before you abandon me for that damn book again?"

She closes her laptop and smiles at me. "Are you jealous of my job, Sam Bradshaw?"

When she stands, I pull her into my arms. "You *do* have your hands on that computer a hell of a lot more often than they're on me." I shrug. "Not complaining. Just pointing out the facts."

She giggles. "You're ridiculous."

"How's it coming?"

She bites down on her lip and cuts her eyes to the computer. "Better than I expected. Her notes are good and her life is *fascinating*. Did you know her husband was verbally abusive?"

I press a kiss to her shoulder. "Mmm-hmm."

"And her father was too, so I'm weaving the two together in this chapter about perseverance. God, I hope she likes it."

Sliding my hands into her hair, I lift my head so I can look into her eyes. "She's liked every other chapter so far, and I'm positive this will be no exception. You're talented and she's lucky as hell you took the job."

Not long after Sabrina was brought up on charges, Christine slipped dramatically in the polls and announced that she'd be stepping aside to let Roe on the ticket so she could focus on her daughter's mental health. Not long later, Christine asked Liz if she'd be interested in ghost-writing her memoirs, and Liz's new career was born.

"So what's for dinner?" Liz asks.

"I promised something special. Why don't you go find out?"

She walks into the dining room and stops when she sees the table set with nothing but champagne glasses and a rose. "Is that a ring in the bottom of my champagne?"

I wrap my arms around her from behind and press a kiss to her neck. "You've been my girl again for almost two months now, but I still feel like I'm dreaming when I wake up beside you."

She turns in my arms and puts her fingertips to my cheeks. "Is this real?"

I swallow hard. "That's what you wanted, right? Something real? Because I didn't used to think I could do that, but then I fell for you and realized I couldn't have it any other way. Life is just *better* with you. Marry me, Elizabeth Thompson. I want to take care of you. I want to put babies in your belly. I want us to grow old holding each other's hand."

"Yes," she breathes. She wraps her arms around my neck and kisses me, but she pulls back before I'm ready. "Did Hanna know you were going to do this? Because she was acting weird at the bakery this morning."

I arch a brow. "You think I'd propose to you without getting Hanna's blessing? I like my nuts, thank you very much."

She giggles, lighting that fire in my chest, and I wrap my arms around her and hold her tight. I never plan on letting go.

THE END

ACKNOWLEDGMENTS

As always, I thank my family first. Brian, thank you for the time, encouragement, and patience you give to me and my books. For sending me to the "satellite office" to work when the kids won't leave me alone, for listening to my endless out-of-context plot concerns, and for proving day after day that happily-ever-after exists outside my head. You and the kids are *my* something real, and I'm grateful.

My friends and family, who celebrate my successes as their own, cheer me on every step of the way, and pimp my books out to every literate adult they meet. I am humbled by your enthusiasm and grateful to have built a life surrounded by such amazing people.

To everyone who provided me feedback on and cheers for Liz and Sam's story along the way—especially Adrienne Hogan, Mira Lyn Kelly, Heather Carver, Karen Newman, and Samantha Leighton—you're all awesome. To Lexi's Midnight Readers, who always lift me up when the words on the page are being difficult. You remind me daily why I love this job so much!

Thank you to the team that helped me package this book and promote it. Sarah Hansen at Okay Creations designed my beautiful cover, and if I have my way she will do many, many more for me. Rhonda Helms and

Lauren McKellar, thank you for the insightful line edits, and Arran McNicol at Editing720 for proofreading. Thanks to my PA, Chris, who does her best to keep me organized, even when we're juggling fifteen tasks at once. A shout-out to Julie of AToMR for your work to promote my books, and to all of the bloggers and reviewers who help her do it. Amazing. Every one of you.

To my agent, Dan Mandel, and my foreign rights agent, Stefanie Diaz, for getting my books into the hands of readers all over the world. Thank you for being part of my team.

To my NWBs—Sawyer Bennett, Lauren Blakely, Violet Duke, Jessie Evans, Melody Grace, Monica Murphy, and Kendall Ryan—y'all rock my world. I'm sure you were ready to strangle me when I was trying to figure out how to approach this series and tell the story in the best way possible. Thank you for always giving it to me straight and handing me the brown paper bag when I'm panicking.

To all my writer friends on Twitter, Facebook, and my various writer loops, thank you for your support and inspiration. I must say, ours is the coolest water cooler in the entire workforce.

And last but certainly not least, thank you to my fans. To those who read the other New Hope books and wanted more, to those who've declared you'd gladly read my grocery lists, and to those who have been with me from the very beginning, thank you. I appreciate each and every one of you. I couldn't do this without you and wouldn't want to. Thank you for buying my books and telling your friends about them. Thank you for asking me to write more. You're the best!

~Lexi

LOVE UNBOUND BY LEXI RYAN

If you enjoyed Liz and Sam's story, I think you'll also enjoy the other books in Love Unbound, the series of books set in New Hope and about the characters you've come to love.

Love Unbound: Splintered Hearts
Unbreak Me (Maggie's story)
Stolen Wishes: A Wish I May Prequel Novella (Will and Cally's prequel)
Wish I May (Will and Cally's novel)
Or read them together in the omnibus edition,
Splintered Hearts: The New Hope Trilogy

Love Unbound: Here and Now
Lost in Me (Hanna's story begins)
Fall to You (Hanna's story continues)
All for This (Hanna's story concludes)
Or read them together in the omnibus edition, *Here and Now: The Complete Series*

Love Unbound: Reckless and Real
Something Wild (Liz and Sam's story begins)
Something Reckless (Liz and Sam's story continues)
Something Real (Liz and Sam's story concludes)

OTHER TITLES BY LEXI RYAN

Hot Contemporary Romance
Text Appeal
Accidental Sex Goddess

Decadence Creek Stories and Novellas
Just One Night
Just the Way You Are

CONTACT LEXI

I love hearing from readers, so find me on my Facebook page at facebook.com/lexiryanauthor, follow me on Twitter @writerlexiryan, shoot me an email at writerlexiryan@gmail.com, or find me on my website: www.lexiryan.com.